FLOOR FOUR

A Novella of
Horror and the Supernatural

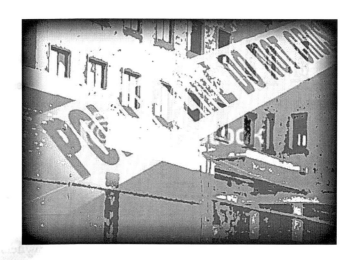

A. LOPEZ, JR.

Ace Hil Ink

FLOOR FOUR
Copyright © 2013 by A. Lopez, Jr.
Published by Ace-Hil-Ink 2013

ISBN-13: 978-0-6157-8797-8
ISBN-10: 0-6157-8797-5

All rights reserved. No parts of this publication may be reproduced, stored in or introduced into a retrieval system, or transmitted in any form, or by any means (electronic, mechanical, photocopying, recording or other forms) without the prior written permission of the copyright owner of this book, except in the case of brief quotations embodied in critical articles and reviews.

This is a work of fiction. Names, characters, places, brands, media and incidents are either the product of the author's imagination or are used fictitiously. The author acknowledges the trademarked status and trademark owners of various products referenced in this work of fiction, which have been used without permission. The publication and or use of these trademarks is not authorized, associated with, or sponsored by the trademark owners.

For any questions about the book or author, please refer to our contact page at: www.ace-hil-ink.com

CONTENTS

"Anyone who sees me, must die!"
~ David Henry Coleman ~

FLOOR FOUR

1

THE MANGLER

The rain continued to pound the top of Mary Tompkins' car as she talked to her husband on the phone. She needed to finish this business dinner, and after that, she would be done for the week and get to spend time at home, while enjoying a long three-day weekend.

Lightning flashed across the sky as she finished her call. Mary took a quick look at the dreary weather as a loud clap of thunder followed and vibrated in her chest. She grabbed her umbrella, opened the door, and a strong gust of wind slapped her face. As she closed the door and set the alarm remote, she heard the sound of rattling chains behind her. Before she could turn around, she felt a sharp, hot pain in her back. Her head shot back as her back was split apart. A gust of rain and wind blew the umbrella from her shaking hand. It happened so fast she couldn't scream, and her eyes closed as she died instantly, while still standing.

The killer held Mary's body upright with his razor-sharp sickle still lodged in her back. He wrapped the heavy chain around her head and neck and pulled the sickle from her back. Her body slumped and the slack in the heavy chain tightened around her neck as she fell. He dragged her to a dark corner of the parking lot next to a vacant lot, and then down a ditch that disappeared into a small creek. Mary's blood stained the path the killer had taken, but it was quickly washed away by the heavy rain.

It was a perfect night to commit a murder—dark, rainy, and very few people out. Mary Tompkins was the eighth victim of serial killer, David Henry Coleman, also known as *The Mangler*. His well-planned and violently executed murders took place in different cities and states, leaving authorities with the difficult task of tracking him. Coleman was a violent serial killer, much more aggressive than most. The FBI described his murders as angry outbursts, but Coleman was never sloppy, and he always left a calling card, making him the most feared serial killer in years. When Coleman killed his victims, he took the bodies to a place where they would easily be found. His calling card was the sickle. In each murder, the victim's face was sliced and cut, beaten, and *mangled* beyond recognition. The sickle would be lodged in the chest, his trademark. It was determined that some of the victims were alive when he sliced their faces. Authorities had their murder weapon, but it never gave them any leads. The Mangler toyed with them and knew exactly what he was doing.

The Mangler's murderous run had gone on for four years. He averaged two killings a year, with his path taking him from the east coast to the Midwest and down south. Mary Tompkins lived in Florida. There was no way to tell when and where he would strike next, and this made it hard to pin him down.

Police got their first break in August of 2002 when they received a call from a resident in Liberty County, Texas. The resident told police a suspicious man had been walking up and down their road late at night. This was a farming community and strangers rarely walked that stretch of road. They sent out a patrol car with the officer treating it as a routine call, but everyone had the serial killer in the back of their minds, especially law enforcement. The police officer didn't find the man or find anything out of the ordinary. A call went out to surrounding counties to be on alert, knowing the serial killer was still out there somewhere.

Coleman chose his victims at random but planned their murders in a very precise way. There was no connection between the victims, no similarities. Half were men and half were women. They ranged from married couples with kids, to single without kids. Those facts, combined with him constantly changing places, left everything unpredictable and everyone on edge. They all waited for him to make an unlikely mistake. The break the police got began with the resident spotting the stranger dressed in black, walking the country road. Without making the communities anxious, law enforcement moved to a higher alert level behind the scenes.

"David Henry Coleman planned his ninth murder in September of 2002, close to the Old River-Lost Lake area here just up the road." The old man began telling the story to the three junior high kids. "A very small, quiet community, Old River found itself in the middle of a major manhunt. Coleman chose the time just after dusk to make his way to the home of a Mark and Jean Ellis. They had just finished working outside around the house and were cleaning up for dinner when Coleman peered into their kitchen window. They didn't see him, they were lucky. The Mangler had not planned this murder like the rest. He rushed it, you see. His need to kill and murder again made him careless. Maybe he wanted more notoriety than he had before or wanted to be taken seriously, but this was his mistake."

The young boys listened closely, their eyes fixed on the man known to the neighborhood kids as, *Old Man Jake*. Jake, an older black man in his sixties, stood tall with a tough demeanor and graying hair. The truth was, he was a gentle giant who enjoyed the simple things in life, most of all, sitting on his porch and smoking a good cigar. He had lived across the road from Saint Vincent Hospital for thirty years and knew the hospital in its heyday when it was the only hospital in town. He saw the demise, as the new times rolled in, and newer buildings were built, all in the name of business and opportunity.

Jake continued, "Coleman watched the married couple get things ready for dinner. His plan was to wait until Mark came back outside, and then use his sickle and chain to end his life. He waited patiently. I imagine a sly smile came over his face as their dinner ended and Mark got up from the table and walked to the back door. Coleman moved into position in the shadows. Mark grabbed a water bucket from the back porch and headed towards the stalls. Coleman waited until Mark entered the stalls and then walked in his direction, but just then, a truck came driving up the dirt road to the house. With the sound of the truck, Mark headed back outside just as Coleman was entering. The killer had no choice but to strike down with the sickle. Shocked, Mark screamed out as the blow from the blade cut into his shoulder. Coleman's momentum carried them into the doorway of the barn, just as the headlights from the truck shined on them. They fell to the ground. Mark struggled in pain as Coleman raised the sickle and prepared to strike down on him again. Mark moved and Coleman missed, as the pointed end of the sickle slammed into the dirt floor. Dust rose all around in the struggle and the long chain clanged to the ground between them. Coleman went to make one last attempt to murder his prey when he heard Jean's screams behind him. He took one last swing with the sickle and hit Mark in the arm, slicing halfway through. Coleman got up, grabbed his chain and ran towards the back of the small barn. The neighbor in the truck, from just down the road, grabbed his shotgun and ran to where Jean was standing. He made it just in time to see Coleman running away. He fired a shot and hit Coleman in the right leg. The shot knocked him forward, but he didn't lose his footing and was able to run outside to the surrounding woods. The bloody sickle was left behind. Mark was the only victim to survive an attack by the famous serial killer. He was taken to a hospital as the manhunt began." Jake paused to let the last part set in.

The three boys, still curious and listening, looked at each other.

Jake leaned forward and continued, "Two things worked in favor for the police you see, the suspect was bleeding, and he had left his murder weapon behind. At this point, they didn't know if it was the Mangler or a copycat, but this man had to be found and arrested. The manhunt continued through the night with helicopters and dogs. They were able to track him in this direction, and around four in the morning, police were dispatched to a neighborhood here in Baytown. A resident spotted a suspicious-looking man walking through the alley, but by the time police arrived, the man was gone. They sealed off the area for four or five miles, and worked their way in."

"Just as dawn broke, another call came in to police just a short distance away from the original call. A resident, taking out his garbage, saw a man sitting in the shrubs across the street. He couldn't give a good description, and again, when police arrived, he was gone. Though this time, the dogs picked up a scent. The helicopter was called in, and the hounds barked and howled louder than you ever heard before." Jake's voice grew loud and animated.

"They were closing in on him. The wooded area led to another neighborhood just on the other side. Not as many people lived in this area and with daylight on their side, the police felt they would find him as they approached from both directions. The hounds closed in on a garage next to a vacant house. After setting a perimeter, they burst into the garage and found some bloody clothes that matched the description Mark Ellis gave them earlier. The suspect was not in the garage, so they focused on the vacant house. They broke through the front and back doors at the same time," he said with excitement building in his voice.

"Gunfire erupted in a back room. The police had no choice but to fire back, hitting the suspect several times. They called an ambulance to save the man, who they suspected to be the Mangler. Paramedics stabilized him on the way to Saint Vincent Hospital," the old man said, as he pointed across the main road. "Right over there."

The boys looked over their shoulders at the old vacant hospital.

"After arriving, Coleman's condition worsened, but not before he told an FBI agent that he was indeed, David Henry Coleman, the Mangler. He confessed to all the murders as two other agents looked on. Coleman's heartless expression showed one of a remorseless murderer."

"A day later, while still in ICU, Coleman's hand began to shake violently." The old man paused in thought, looking down at the ground. "The nurse walked over to him, just in reach of his handcuffed wrist, and he quickly grabbed her arm. He looked her in the eye and said, *'I will be back, and I will return, and kill again and again. I will haunt this place forever!'* They say his eyes stayed open, staring at the nurse until he died. She screamed and broke away from his death grip. The FBI rushed in, but Coleman was already dead." Jake paused, making the boys wait a little longer. "You know, they say he walks the halls of the old hospital carrying his sickle and dragging his chain. The anniversary of his death is coming up this week."

Old Man Jake knew how to tell a story. He sat back in his chair and lit his half-smoked cigar.

"That's the story of the Mangler."

The three, wide-eyed thirteen-year-olds, sat on their bikes, staring at Jake. Two of them, Doug and Kyle, heard stories from him before, but it never got old. The other boy, Brandon, was new in town. They brought him to Jake's so he could hear the tale of the Mangler.

After hearing Jake tell his story, the boys headed out on their bikes towards the hospital. But not without one last word from Jake.

"Y'all be careful now," he said, as he took one last puff from his cigar before dropping it on the ground and smothering it under his shoe.

The boys, way up the sidewalk by then, waved back as they sped off.

"Best be careful," Jake said quietly to himself, knowing kids rarely listened to advice from adults.

Jake loved telling the story of the serial killer to the neighborhood kids. He did it to scare the kids so they would stay away from the old hospital, knowing the killer's ghost haunted the building on the anniversary of his death. He knew he couldn't stop the kids from sneaking in and out, but he would make sure they couldn't get in on the anniversary of Coleman's death. Since Jake lived near the hospital, he enjoyed taking walks to the park behind it. The walks helped him free his mind of his late wife, who passed away three short years ago. The gazebo was his favorite place to visit in the park. The octagonal-shaped structure was set out over the water, about thirty feet from land. A nice cool breeze usually blew across the open water and through the gazebo. Jake enjoyed watching the kids play basketball on the concrete courts and the sounds of the younger kids laughing on the playground. This was his place to get away from it all, at least for a short time, but he hadn't taken his normal walks in the last few days because of the recent thunderstorms.

He never told the kids, that *he* was the one who called police when he spotted Coleman in the alley that day. He didn't know it then, but that was the beginning of his personal attachment to the murderer. He had never been visited by Coleman's ghost at home, so he figured it only existed inside the walls of the hospital. After all, he was responsible for getting him shot. Jake figured if there was anyone he was going to hunt and seek out for revenge, it would be him. The anniversary of Coleman's death was coming Saturday, and he planned to keep his usual routine—walking around the old building and making sure the door the kids used to get inside, was locked. This was Jake's yearly ritual.

Built in the late 1940s, Saint Vincent Hospital stood tall at five stories, overlooking the small town. At the time, it was a massive hospital, covering over 280,000 square feet, staying in business until 2004, when its ownership completed the transition to a modern version of the hospital, built on the other side of town. Since the closure of the original hospital, there have been reports of it being haunted. A private business used the building for a short period after its closure. Most reports of hauntings came from the staff and late-night security guards. The old building was finally shut down in 2006 and sits on top of a small hill, giving it a more massive look and feel. At dusk and set against the western sky, its dark and menacing appearance fueled speculation of the place being haunted. To keep trespassers out, the windows were boarded up, and a fence was put up along the edge of the property.

Not too long after, the property owners hired a contract company to do some minor, structural repair work on the lower level. Just as the three-week project was about to end, contract worker Ed Payton was found one morning, hung to death, hanging from a chain on an overhead rafter. There was no suicide note, or any reason in his personal life to hang himself, and investigators ruled it a homicide. Rumors of the Mangler still haunting the building escalated, especially since a chain was used, one of his trademark tools. There was no stool, no box, or ladder for Ed Payton to climb up on to do it himself. He just hung freely in his work clothes, his feet more than five feet from the ground, and rumors circulated of his face being filled with terror when he was found. After the investigation, more fencing was put in place to secure the grounds. But during the summers, it was hard to keep kids like, Doug, Kyle, and now Brandon, from finding ways in and exploring. High school kids showed no fear and were always being run out of the area by police.

David Henry Coleman died on the fourth floor in ICU—that floor is said to be most haunted. People have reported hearing chains rattling and the sound of metal scraping in the shadows. Rumors can be exaggerated, but when a haunting is suspected, the reported sounds are much more believable. An assessment of structural integrity was required for the building once a year, and over that time only once has anyone reported anything strange. A city inspector on the fourth floor said she heard noises coming from near the old ICU hall. She walked further down the dark hall with a flashlight in her hands and heard the sound of a chain dragging on the floor. That scared her enough to turn around and head back down to the first floor. She wouldn't go back up, even after her coworkers searched the area and found nothing. Not many dared to go up there after that.

Doug and Kyle took Brandon to the back of the hospital so he could see the *scary* side of it. Even in the middle of the day, the hospital took on an ominous look. The backside of the hospital was where the curious would sneak in through a hole in the fence. Brandon stood, straddling his bike, with one foot on the ground and he scanned the building from top to bottom. Doug and Kyle rode their bikes around the fencing to the far corner, and he quickly jumped up on his seat and peddled towards them. A large covered patio served as the back entrance to the hospital and the covered area provided shade from the evening sun, creating a makeshift break area for employees—a couple of the concrete tables and chairs still stood there. The boys hid their bikes behind some overgrown shrubs and went in through their *secret* spot.

"You're pretty brave, Brandon. I never made it this far my first time," Doug said.

"Quit trying to scare him," Kyle said. "It's okay, nothing to be scared of," Kyle said to Brandon, as they walked further in. The patio was at least sixty feet wide and another forty feet to the back entrance. Despite the afternoon sun, the covered patio cast dark shadows in the far corners. They stopped a few feet from the back entrance. The owners had the doors boarded with plywood and locked with chains.

"Most people think you can't get in, but we know a way. Want to go in?" Doug asked as he looked at Brandon.

14

Brandon was usually game for things like this, but he was a little nervous with Doug pushing him to go further. "Yeah, let's go," Brandon, said. Kyle looked on. They had done this a few times before, and it was always fun to show someone the *haunted* hospital for the first time.

Doug led them to a corner where the walls intersected and disappeared behind a sheet of plywood. Brandon and Kyle waited for a moment before Doug reappeared smiling. "We can still get in." He promptly disappeared again and they followed him through an old rusty door that opened just enough, allowing them to pass through.

The dark and damp hall smelled like sewage.

The boys frowned at the smell, temporarily holding their breath.

Doug and Kyle turned on their flashlights revealing the graffiti-lined walls in various colors and styles. Some represented gangs, some professed their love, and others were just there in the form of street-art. They could hear water dripping at the end of the hallway, most likely from the recent rainstorm.

"Still looks the same as before. The fourth floor is where the Mangler died," Doug said, looking at Brandon. "The only way to get up there is through the stairs down the hall."

He pointed the flashlight towards the stairwell. Brandon's heart beat fast with excitement, but still leery now that they were inside. Shining their lights in all directions, they walked towards the end of the hall. Old shards of metal and pipes, detached wiring, and broken Sheetrock filled the floor and forced them to walk in a weaving pattern as they closed in on the door to the stairwell. Despite Doug's brave appearance, he stayed close to the other two.

Finally, they were at the door. "Here it is," Doug said. He pushed the door, and surprisingly, it swung easily on its hinges. The metal door, covered in rust, came to a creaking stop, revealing the entrance to the stairwell which looked like a black hole. They stepped forward and shined their lights on every wall and corner, casting eerie shadows in every direction.

"You ready to go up?" Doug asked, just as scared as them. They nodded without taking their eyes off the stairs above. Kyle held tight to his flashlight as Doug led the way, with Brandon trailing Kyle. Once they got to the second floor, Doug paused. "Shhh, just checking to see if we can hear his chain dragging on the floor."

"Come on, Doug, quit trying to scare him," Kyle said.

"There's nothing to be scared of until we get to the fourth floor anyway," Doug said with a laugh.

"Have you ever been to the fourth floor?" Brandon asked them.

"No, not—" Kyle began to say before Doug cut him off.

"Sure, many times. We've never seen the Mangler, but we know he's there."

A loud bang came from above, scaring them, and they quickly shined their lights up the stairwell. The sound of something falling down the stairs followed before everything went dead silent. They continued looking up and noticed something stirring the dust above—the particles of dust floated across the beams of their lights like tiny snowflakes. Someone or some *thing* was up there. Doug walked up a couple of more steps, sweat forming on his forehead. Kyle and Brandon looked at him, their feet locked into place, they had no intention of going any further.

"Probably just a cat or something," Doug said. He took another step up and craned his head at an awkward angle to see what had stirred the dust.

"Maybe we should go, Doug, it's too dark," Kyle said.

"No, I want to see the Mangler," Doug said in a deep haunting voice, trying to scare them.

Just as he finished his sentence and began to laugh, the unmistakable sound of a dragging chain from above wiped the grin off Doug's face. Frozen in place, and listening intently, the boys heard the sound of the chain dropping slowly, one step after another. They looked at each other with the same look of, *Let's get the hell out of here!*

Their flashlights no longer shined above, they didn't want to see what was coming, but the dusty light shining on their faces showed the fear they could no longer hide. The sound of the chain grew louder, getting closer. Then came the high-pitched sound of metal grinding against metal.

The boys turned and ran down the stairwell to the first floor and straight to the door they entered earlier. In the boy's minds, the sound of the metal grinding on the handrails had to be the Mangler's sharpened sickle. There were no words between them as they squeezed out the door, all thinking the exact same thing . . . *Get Out!*

Brandon was the last one out, but couldn't help looking down the hall to the stairway door. Just as he made his last push to slide out, he saw the doors to the stairs being pushed open. He yelled, turned away, and ran to his bike.

Seniors in high school, Russell, Jesse, Craig, and Christy, had been friends since fifth grade. They did the normal high school parties and get-togethers, but for the most part stayed away from trouble. They hung out with other friends but kept close to their own little circle. One thing they did like doing for kicks was sneaking into the old hospital. They had done it three or four times, but never went deep into the upper floors. They loved testing the rumors of the haunting by wandering around the first floor, and most recently, going to the spot where the worker was hung. Russell and Jesse were teammates on the varsity football team and kept their options open on the dating scene, while Craig and Christy were dating and looked forward to going to college together.

With the anniversary of the Mangler's death coming up over the weekend, they had plans to throw a private party on the fourth floor with some friends. None of them had ever been to the fourth floor, but figured, as a group, it would be fun and adventurous, and a lot safer than going alone. Russell and Jesse were letting only a handful of close friends know about the party. They didn't want to have too many people there, or for anyone to find out, especially the police. Their plan was to have a keg of beer, some food, and music and they also planned to have a few flashlights and candles to make sure there was plenty of light. With Russell, Jesse, Craig, and a couple of other guys, along with the girls, they wouldn't have any trouble getting all of their party décors up there on one trip. He looked forward to the party and playing a joke on some of the partygoers with Jesse, but they needed to sneak into the hospital before the party to set up some pranks to scare everyone. It was Friday afternoon and their plans were going well. Keeping it a secret was a must.

Doug woke up Saturday and rode his bike the short distance to Kyle's house. Kyle was just getting out of bed.

"Why are you up so early?" Kyle asked as Doug sat down at Kyle's computer desk.

"Guess what I heard? Russell and some of the other guys are planning a party for tonight," Doug said, excitement beaming on his face.

"So? They always have parties on the weekends. What's the difference?"

"The difference is that this party is gonna be at the old hospital, on the fourth floor."

Doug watched Kyle's reaction.

"Are you serious? They plan on having it there?" Kyle looked surprised, his eyes sparkled with anticipation.

"Yes, I heard my sister talking on the phone about it. It starts at ten tonight. I think we should go around ten-thirty and sneak in," Doug said proudly.

"I don't know, Doug. How will we be able to stay out that late without getting in trouble with our parents?"

"Simple." Doug already had a plan. "We say we are spending the night at Brandon's, and he says he is staying at one of our houses." Proud of his plan, Doug smiled.

"I don't know if that will work. Did you ask Brandon?"

"No, but I will this morning."

"What about all those noises we heard when we were there? You were just as scared as us," Kyle said.

"Come on. Do you want to do it or not? Russell and the rest will be there anyway. Nothing to be scared of, right?" said Doug, doing his best to convince Kyle.

"Okay, if you can get Brandon to go along, I'll go."

Kyle tried to hide his excitement, but if Doug could make it work, he knew it would be a fun night. The only question was . . . who made those noises in the stairs the last time?

The party was set to start at ten, so Russell and Jesse planned to meet at the hospital just after dark to take some things inside, set up for the party, and plan their pranks. The day darkened earlier than usual because of a thunderstorm in the afternoon that left the skies cloudy and overcast the rest of the day.

Russell and Jesse arrived at the back entrance to the hospital in Jesse's truck. Chairs, a table, and a small sound system for the music, filled the truck's bed.

"We'll have to take this stuff in two loads. The truck should be okay parked here," Russell said.

The faded, dark blue paint on the truck blended in well with the dark bushes.

"Yeah, we just need to be quick," said Jesse. He was excited about the party, and the possibility of having some fun with the rest of the group that night.

They grabbed the table and chairs first. As they made their way to the hidden entrance, they noticed the door was open. They always closed the door when they left. This meant either someone was inside or someone had just left. They pushed through with more caution than usual. Russell carried the four chairs, two in each hand. Jesse held the plastic table at his side as they moved along the first room towards the stairway. Both carried flashlights, with Jesse holding his light with his free hand. After a bit of a struggle, they were standing at the stairwell door. The old door was also open, when it was usually closed, they looked at each other, but then laughed it off. They were scaring themselves before they could even pull the pranks on their friends.

Jesse entered first and shined his light along the stairs as they walked one step at a time to the next floor. Their shoes slid against the grit and dust with each step crushing the dry debris, awakening the dead-quiet stairwell. The boys tried to break up the awkward silence by joking about the upcoming night, but as they got to the third floor, Jesse stopped suddenly. Russell, trailing, bumped into him.

"What happened? What's wrong?" he asked.

"I don't know. I thought I heard something."

"Come on. Now you're sounding like a scared little girl. Keep going," Russell said.

Unaware something stirred above them on the steps, he nudged Jesse in his back to move him forward.

"Listen! Can't you hear it?" asked Jesse. His heart beat fast. His eyes focused on the beam of light shining above. Russell also looked, but neither could see the culprit. For a moment, dead silence washed over the stairwell just before the sounds started again—now the unmistakable sound of a chain dragging on the concrete floor. Russell didn't show his fear, but his heart beat just as fast as Jesse's. Russell set the chairs down and grabbed his flashlight. He shined it alongside Jesse's light but they could only see dust particles floating in and out of the railings leading to the fourth floor. The clanging chains grew louder, getting closer. The boys froze, but Russell found some bravado, despite his fear.

"Who's there?" he demanded. "You better show yourself or we'll kick your ass!" The sound of the dragging chains stopped one flight of stairs above them.

More silence.

The chains rattled again—the source of the noise was about to reveal itself. The boys wanted to run, their minds told them they had to run, but they couldn't. Their hands shook, causing the beams of light to dance around the walls like strobe lights at a party. Only, their party hadn't started yet.

Or had it?

"I said, who's there?" Russell asked once more, in a less than demanding tone. The uncontrolled shaking of his hand showed his fear. The unknown scared him shitless, but his stubborn determination kept him in place. He had to see what was there.

In the darkness, they could see a hand holding the dangling chain coming around the turn. The flashlights beamed through the specks of dust and simultaneously, both lights shined in the face of the man carrying the chains.

They recognized the man, to their shock and relief.

"You boys better quit messing around in here." It was Old Man Jake, holding the heavy chains. "It's too dangerous in here to be playing around." Jake stopped and shined his light down the stairway at the boys. They stood in silence. "What are you boys planning? What's all that for?"

Russell spoke, "We were just gonna have a party up here tonight. It won't hurt nothin'.." His anxiety gone, once he realized it was only Jake.

"That's not a good idea. The floors upstairs aren't good. You boys leave this chain lying around?" Jake lifted the brand new chain and walked down the stairs towards them. "Get that light out of my face, and you boys best be heading home." He walked past them as they moved out of his way.

Russell and Jesse didn't know how to respond. Even at his age, Jake could be intimidating when he wanted and took one more step past them before turning around. "This building is old. Listen to what I tell you." He turned and walked down to the second floor. The old man's serious tone settled in their minds for a moment as they heard him work his way down.

They looked at each other. Russell didn't show concern, but Jesse had his confidence shaken. "I don't care what he said. We're still having this party. He just came down from the fourth floor and nothing happened. Everything will be fine," Russell said.

"I know what you're saying, it's just kinda weird. What was he doing in here anyway?" Jesse asked.

Russell couldn't come up with a good answer.

"I don't know. Maybe he has a thing for old buildings. Who knows? All I know is, we're having this party no matter what," Russell said, as he turned off his flashlight and grabbed the chairs. He started moving up to the fourth floor as Jesse, his flashlight still in hand, reluctantly followed him.

Despite Jake's warning, Russell and Jesse continued up to the fourth floor and set up the tables and chairs. They figured, if Old Man Jake was able to walk alone on the fourth floor, they surely would be safe with their group of friends up there later. After they finished setting up, they left and made phone calls to everyone who was invited. They let the *select* few know the party was still on.

But Jesse's head rang again with the question, *what was Jake doing up here?*

Jake hid a secret and a unique relationship with the Mangler and the old hospital. No one he told the stories to, especially the kids, knew he worked at the hospital for a short time. He had a part-time job there doing odd jobs and delivering the inner-office mail throughout the hospital. Jake worked on the fourth floor the day after David Henry Coleman was admitted to the hospital, allowing him access to the ICU to deliver documents and mail.

He had to pass Coleman's room to get to the nurse's station that day. As he walked by, he glanced at the two FBI agents, who stood at his doorway in the typical government style, looking straight ahead through dark shades, with hands crossed in front. After dropping the paperwork at the nurse's station, Jake made his way back down the hall and glanced into Coleman's room. Coleman's eyes were closed, wires and tubes attached all over his body, and as he was about to walk away, David Henry Coleman suddenly opened his eyes and looked directly at Jake. The intense gaze frightened Jake, as Coleman raised his cuffed hand as far as he could and pointed at Jake. And through all the wires and hoses running in and out of the killer's body, his eyes strained and grew more intense, saying, *I'll get you!*

Jake broke from the hypnotic trance and quickly walked away. Down the hall, he heard a nurse scream and a computerized voice came over the hospital speaker system calling the staff to Coleman's room as his body failed.

Jake learned soon after, Coleman had died. That one moment Jake had with the serial killer, no matter how brief, would haunt him and connect the two men years after—a secret he always kept to himself. This was the reason he walked the hospital floors after it was shut down. He needed to face his fears and not let Coleman take his mind. The experience he had that day scared Jake, but he exorcised the demon every time he walked on the fourth floor of the old hospital. He knew its ghost would haunt the floors on the anniversary of his death. He had seen Coleman five times, each time they stood opposing each other in the hall, only it wasn't Coleman anymore, it was the Mangler who stood there, chain in one hand, sickle in the other. He would stand and laugh loudly down the hall as if he knew something no one else knew. The first time Jake saw him, he was paralyzed by the same fear that had grabbed him years earlier. He knew it wasn't just trying to scare him, because each time the killer laughed, he would stop suddenly and point his finger at Jake as he did before. Then, as he gave him that same demonic stare, the Mangler would slowly fade away into the darkness like magic . . . dark magic. Jake planned to take this secret to his grave. He wasn't concerned about the stories he told to the kids, he knew they were safe, even if they got curious and ventured in the old hospital. But he made sure no one could get in on the anniversary of his death. He felt a responsibility to protect the public and the property—as long as he was able to confront the monster in the hall, and until it faded away as it did each time. He knew the stories made the kids more curious and would seek answers, but he really wanted to put so much fear in them, they would stay away.

He held some kind of power over Coleman and it kept the killer in the spirit world. The only time Jake failed to make the anniversary walk was the week the construction worker was murdered. Knowing the kids planned to have a party, he had to make sure they couldn't get in through that door. He had to keep them out.

Jake went back to the hospital a little after dark and picked up the chain he had brought down earlier and used it to secure the door with a padlock. There was no way he was going to let those kids fall into any danger goofing around in the hospital, especially that night. After he locked the door, he had a look around and didn't see anyone lingering on the property, and went home.

2

R.S.V.P.

Doug and Kyle got Brandon to go along with their plan—a little peer pressure can go a long way. The plan was for them to lie to their parents and say they were staying at the other's house for the night. To fool their parents, they would actually stay at a relative of Doug's. Brandon was the least sure of the idea, but went along, trying to fit in. The noises they heard earlier at the old hospital were forgotten, as the excitement about the party grew.

The sun faded into the western sky, and darkness consumed the town. Kyle and Doug were at his cousin's house and waiting to hear from Brandon. They were getting excited about crashing the party and finally getting to go up to the famous fourth floor. Kyle worried that Brandon would screw up their plans.

"Maybe we shouldn't have let Brandon know what we were going to do. He might tell on us, and we'll all get in trouble," said Kyle.

"He'll make it. He wants to check it out as much as we do." Doug didn't have faith in Brandon showing up either, but he wasn't going to let Kyle know, or he might back out too.

Brandon sat at home, nervous, and had a bad feeling about the party. He looked forward to his first year of high school and didn't want to ruin it by getting in trouble, but at the same time, he didn't want to lose his new friends in Doug and Kyle. He still had a little time to decide before his mother would get suspicious and start asking questions. The hospital was only a five-minute ride on his bike, just in case he wanted to meet them there later.

Russell and the rest of the partygoers showed up around nine that night after Russell and Jesse set up a couple of pranks for later. They had a couple of friends drop them off with the keg of beer, coolers full of food, flashlights, candles and whatever else they needed for the party. The friends parked their vehicles just down the street at the twenty-four-hour grocery store, then walked back.

Jesse made it to the door first and saw the chain and lock.

"Damn!"

Russell walked up behind him. "What's wrong? Door locked?" Russell began to laugh.

"What's so funny? We can't get in now."

"I figured the old man would do something like this. I expected it. But, I know another way in," Russell said, with a smile.

"What? Another way?" Jesse had never known of any other way to get in.

"Yeah. Not many know about the entrance in the delivery area. You have to go down some steps to get to the door."

"And you never told me?" Jesse seemed offended.

"I never had a reason to tell anyone, as long as we could always get in through here," Russell said as he tapped on the lock with his flashlight. "Besides, my older brother told me about it, and made me swear to not tell anyone."

Without another word, they walked back to their friends. Jesse wasn't satisfied with the explanation, but it didn't matter right then, it was time to get the party started. As they got back to the group, Russell was all smiles.

"Looks like we have to use Plan B."

They grabbed their things and headed down the steps to the delivery area on the lower floor.

They made it through the lower entry, just as Russell had told them. Their climb to the fourth floor was a little bit of a walk, but no one complained. They were there to have a good time.

Doug checked the time, it was getting late. "He's not coming. I don't care what he tells you on those text messages," Doug said, "we're gonna have to go alone and hope he doesn't get us in trouble."

"You think we should still go?" Kyle wasn't as *into* the plan as he was before.

"Yeah, it'll be fun," Doug said, as he put his phone back in his pocket.

The boys got some things together and planned to leave, not expecting to hear from Brandon.

Doug and Kyle rode their bikes in and out of the soft amber glow of the street lamps down Memorial Drive on their way to the hospital. Once they made the turn west on Memorial, the dark, ominous five-story hospital towered in front of them. They had seen it this way many times before, but this time, it took on a completely different look and feel. They stopped peddling and let their bikes glide towards the main road, knowing if everything worked out, they were going to see the fourth floor for the first time.

After they made it to the back of the hospital, they hid their bikes and walked to the door.

"Look! It's locked!" Doug said. A look of despair and disappointment came over his face.

Kyle walked around Doug and shook the chain and lock as if it would make a difference. "There has to be another way in. They had to have found a way in," said Doug, as he looked around the building.

They walked a short distance to the side of the building and Doug grabbed Kyle, holding him still to keep him quiet. He spotted two older kids walking down the steps to a lower level. They carried a couple of bags, as they joked and laughed. Doug smiled, knowing they had found their way in.

They waited a bit, then worked their way through the shadows to the stairs leading down to a place they had not been before. Kyle reached into his pocket and pulled out his flashlight.

Doug looked back at Kyle, smiling. "Even if Brandon decides to come he won't be able to get in now, too bad for him." He let out a soft chuckle.

Once they made it to the bottom, they peered into the darkness through the half-open door. They listened for the other two kids until the coast was clear.

The feeling of betrayal, even for a thirteen-year-old kid, was too much to take. Doug and Kyle weren't answering his messages, so Brandon decided to sneak out and ride his bike to meet them at the hospital. The bike ride to the hospital would only take a few minutes.

"I might be able to catch them before they go in," he said to himself, peddling faster.

The party was going well and the music was loud. They had enough candles and flashlights to give the Floor Four hallway a festive but morbid atmosphere. No one down below should be able to hear them and with most of the windows boarded up, no one would be able to see the lights at ground level.

Russell and Jesse overlooked the party in progress and smiled, proud they had pulled it off. There were eight kids altogether, and some were dressed in black, with small chains hanging from their necks as a tribute to the anniversary of the Mangler's death. For most of the high school kids, believing the ghost of the famous serial killer actually haunted the halls was just a myth, or they would not be there. One girl, Linda, wasn't so sure about the stories being a myth and had to see for herself. Russell was waiting for a couple of more friends who were running late and would be there soon.

Smoke rose from the tip of Jake's cigar as he sat on his porch and glanced over at the front of the hospital, noticing nothing unusual. Every time he fired up a cigar, he thought of his late wife and how she detested him smoking, and the awful smell it brought. He didn't smoke too often when she was alive, trying to respect her wishes and her genuine concern for his health. As he sat and thought of everything, he looked at his watch—10:25—not realizing it was that late. He needed to take one last walk for the night and check on the chain and lock he had put on the hospital door.

Carrying his flashlight, Jake made his way through the fence and into the plaza at the back of the hospital. Lightning lit up the sky to the west, the rain wouldn't be long now. He carefully walked the path leading up to the door and was pleased to see the lock and chain were still in place. Jake turned and began to walk towards the fence when he thought he heard the sound of music. He stopped to listen closer and discovered the sound was coming from a broken window above.

Jake walked around the corner and the music grew a louder—nothing that could be heard by anyone driving on the main road, but loud enough from where he stood. His emotions went from satisfied, to anger and fear.

How in the hell did they get in? He knew what was at stake, and he knew these kids had no idea of the danger they were in. He needed to take action, now.

Brandon made it to the hospital and parked his bike next to a tree. He reached for his flashlight and realized he had forgotten it.

Too late now, he thought.

At a brisk pace, he got to the door the boys had shown him earlier, but to his shock, it was chained shut. He did the customary, *grab-and-pull,* but it wasn't budging. Lost on what to do, he contemplated going back home, when he caught a flash of light out of the corner of his eye. At first, he was cautious, thinking it might be the police, but his curiosity got the best of him and he quietly walked in that direction.

Brandon walked towards the light and stopped in the shadows at the steps leading down to the lower level, but without a flashlight there was no way he was going to go down there. His curiosity and the sound of the music kept him from leaving, knowing his friends were in there somewhere.

Suddenly a light flashed from behind!

"What are you doing around here this late at night?" The voice scared Brandon, and he turned quickly to see who it was.

Jake.

"I told you boys, to stay away from here. It's too dangerous to be in there," Jake said.

Brandon trembled with Jake looming over him and his light shining in his eyes. He wanted to turn and run and go back home. "I'm sorry, sir. I was just looking for my friends," Brandon said, as tears welled in his eyes.

"Look, son, you best go home now. I'll find your friends and get them home too. I didn't mean to scare you, but I had to see if you knew the way into the building."

"The only way I know is the way we went in before, but it's locked," said Brandon.

"I know it's locked, I'm the one who did it. Now it sounds like they found another way in." Jake pointed his light to the steps leading down. "You go home. I'll get them out of there before it's too late."

Brandon was scared, he nodded and turned, then walked away towards his bike. Jake shined the light along the path to help him find his way back. He continued walking until he was out of the old man's sight, then crouched down and walked back to follow Jake, making sure he stayed close to his light. Although he was afraid, he knew he had to see what was up there, and prove to his friends that he wasn't a coward.

Everyone invited to the party had made it in, and now it was time for Russell and Jesse to put their pranks in motion. A total of twelve kids were enjoying the music, food, and drinks. The candles cast an eerie glow up and down the hall and circled the main party area just outside the room where the Mangler died. Russell and Jesse had to slip out one at a time to dawn their props for the big scare. They had planned on waiting until midnight, but they didn't know how long the party would last, or if the police would crash it, so they decided now was the time. Russell had placed a good length of chain and a sickle in Coleman's old ICU room. He planned to sneak in there and jump out at the party at just the right time. Jesse was to sneak away down the long hall and get his hidden sickle and chain, along with a mask and walk towards the party group to get their attention just before Russell jumped out at them from behind.

Down below, Doug and Kyle made their way to the third floor without any problems. Their excitement grew as they heard the music just one floor up. They would finally get to see the famous fourth floor and hang out with the older high school kids. Their blind excitement had blocked out their fear of what might be lurking above. The door leading to the third-floor hall was half-open on their left. Doug shined his light into the darkness.

"We better get up to the next floor," said Kyle.

"We will. Don't you want to look around a little bit? We've never been up this far before," Doug said. He pushed the door open to get a better look. "Besides, the party is just getting started," he said, looking back at Kyle. He walked into the pitch-black, third-floor hallway. Kyle looked around with no choice but to follow.

Russell and Jesse slipped away from the party and got in position to scare the others. The sickle and chain were just where Jesse had left them. Russell went straight to where he had left his props. He anxiously looked around the room, they were gone, leaving him puzzled. Someone at the party must have found them, but it was too late now. They had to go on without them, and he hoped that Jesse's chain and sickle were still there. He sent a text to Jesse to start their plan.

Jesse put on the mask and the bloody butcher's apron and grabbed his sickle and chain. He was a good way down the hall, and started his walk towards the unsuspecting partygoers. No one noticed him at first, but halfway down the hall, a girl saw something moving slowly towards them in and out of the shadows.

The lights and candles gave off an eerie glow through Jesse's mask as he methodically walked towards the group. The girl who spotted him froze at first, then turned to the others.

"Look! Who is that?"

Everyone turned and looked in silence at the slow-moving figure as the sound of the dragging chain clanged on the floor. The sickle came into clearer view, raised high, as he approached the outer circle of the lights.

"Oh, my God!" one girl screamed. The entire group backed up slowly, and as they did, they moved directly in front of Russell's hiding place. He waited patiently, ready to jump out at them from behind.

"Who are you? What do you want?" Craig said as he stood out in front of the scared group. "Is this some kind of joke?" he demanded.

"Let's get out of here!" another girl shouted.

Just as the screams and shrieks became louder, Russell made his surprise entrance, jumping out from behind with a scream made for Hollywood, just as Jesse ran towards them at full speed with his sickle and chain. Russell's sudden leap left the group no choice but to run in the darkness down the opposite end of the hall. Craig took one last look, before realizing it was only Russell.

"Son of a bitch!" he yelled. "What the hell is wrong with you?"

Russell and Jesse began to laugh as Jesse took off his mask. Furious, Craig walked up to Jesse and pushed him in the chest, knocking him back a couple of feet.

"What the hell?" he said again, his eyes on fire.

"It's just a joke, man, just a joke," Russell said, "Lighten up."

The rest of the party saw the scuffle and slowly made their way back up the dark hall. Some laughed, while others were just as upset as Craig.

Once everyone was back, Russell apologized, despite a couple of people clapping in appreciation of the joke.

"Sorry, everyone, we didn't mean to scare you. Well, maybe we did, but we didn't want to ruin the party, only to have fun."

Craig and a couple of others were still angry, but stayed and listened.

"He's right," Jesse said, as he stepped forward. "We just wanted to have some fun and figured that we were all here in honor of the Mangler. That's why we did it."

The group slowly let go of their anger as they listened.

"Really, it was just in fun," said Russell.

Victor, a linebacker on the football team and a friend of Jesse, walked up to him, grabbed the chain from his hand, and raised it. "I'll let you slide, this time, but if you pull some shit like that again, I'll strangle you with this chain myself," he said. He raised the chain to Jesse's neck and looked him in the eye. "Just a joke, right?"

The group remained silent, the tension rising. Victor and Jesse smiled, and the tension was broken.

No matter how mad some of them were, the party would still go on. Relieved, Russell patted the linebacker on the shoulder. Victor placed the chain around his own neck and walked away.

Russell looked at Jesse. "That was great, but I didn't think they would be so mad."

"Where is your chain?" Jesse asked him.

"I don't know. I thought you grabbed them, or someone at the party found them, but they weren't where I left them."

"Let's go look," Jesse said.

The party continued as if nothing happened. All was forgiven, glad it was *just* a joke, giving them a false sense of security.

Doug and Kyle walked the hallway on the third floor shining their lights in all directions. The dark corridor looked much like the rest of the hospital. They had just heard screaming from the party above and froze in place, listening. The screams continued and the hairs on the back of their necks stood up, realizing everything they heard *was* real—that fact scared them even more. The boys turned and ran to the door as fast as they could. Just as they made it there, the door slammed shut in their face. Dust and debris flew into the air and floated through the beams of their flashlights. They yelled and pounded on the metal door not knowing who or what, slammed it closed.

Jake walked into the lower level of the loading dock and was surprised to find out there was another way to get in— he thought he knew every inch of the place—and he also knew trouble was coming for those kids above. He carried his flashlight and kept his crowbar ready, knowing Coleman would be waiting for him. He had to get those kids out of there before Coleman had a chance to cross over to the real world and kill again. He heard the faint sound of screams echoing from the party. He hurried his pace, climbing the stairs back up to the first floor from the basement. Once he got to the main level, he went to the stairwell and made the ascent, one step at a time.

Halfway to the second floor, he stopped to catch his breath, when he heard a door slam. He shined his light up the stairwell, but couldn't see anything. He hesitated, hoping the screams were just part of the party's fun. He took a deep breath.

Bang! Bang! Bang! The banging on the door startled Jake.

"Let us out! Let us out!" Doug and Kyle screamed from behind the door.

Jake made it to the door. "Who's in there? Is that you kids?" Jake asked.

"Yes, it's Doug and Kyle. Is that you, Jake?" Doug asked, his voice shaky.

"What the hell are you boys doing in here? I told you to stay away, didn't I?" Jake said, anger building in his voice. He reached for the door handle and tried twisting it, but it wouldn't budge. Jake leaned against the door and pushed, it budged a little. "Pull the door!" he yelled.

The boys pulled as he pushed until the door gave way, creaking loudly as it opened. The three beams of light intersected between them. Jake saw the fear in their eyes— they saw the anger in his.

Brandon heard the commotion in the stairwell above at the same time as Jake. He stopped, straining his eyes to see what was happening. The only thing he could see were beams of light flashing in all directions. Beyond the commotion, he could hear the sound of music and laughter coming from the party above. He continued his ascent, staying as stealth as possible, when he heard Jake shouting at someone.

"You boys get out of here now. Understand me?" Jake said, not asking, but telling.

"Yes... Yes, sir." After being locked in, Doug and Kyle were scared enough and thankful to get the hell out of there. They ran down the stairs towards the second floor. Brandon heard them coming, but he didn't want them to see him just yet, so he ran down a few steps and ducked just inside the second-floor hall. He wanted to prove to them he wasn't afraid, that he *was* there, but at that moment, he had to follow Jake and see what was on the fourth floor.

The boys ran by, never noticing Brandon hiding behind the second-floor door.

Brandon didn't realize how much he was shaking until the boys had rumbled down the stairs on their way out to safety. He came out and quickly made his way back up, closer to Jake and his light.

Victor, after making his point to Russell and Jesse, walked down the hall, the chain still dangling around his neck, on his way to the restroom. Although there was no running water, the kids did use the actual restrooms when they had to go. Victor, feeling brave, walked with his flashlight and found the toilet stalls, along with the terrible smell. He smiled—he was in the right place.

He propped the flashlight so he could see the toilet. An eerie feeling of being watched came over him—his intuition was right. The chain dangling around his neck and over his shoulders was pulled from behind. Startled, Victor tried to turn.

"Hey! What the hell? Don't you see I'm trying to take a piss here?" he said, thinking it was a joke. The chain tightened around his neck and was yanked back violently, Victor's upper body flew backward and the flashlight fell to the floor. He tried to keep his feet planted, just as the coaches taught him in football practice, but the person pulling him was very strong . . . too strong. His air was quickly cut off as he tried desperately to breathe, grabbing at the big chain around his neck.

"Come on, quit playing!" he cried.

His adversary quickly turned him around.

His eyes bulged in their sockets as he was choked and close to death. He saw the person strangling him was not one of his friends.

38

The Mangler struck down with his sickle and drove it straight into Victor's chest. The razor-sharp tip easily sliced its way in and lodged in cartilage and bone. Victor, eyes still bulging and in shock, had no time to react. Coleman stepped away, loosening his grip on the chain and let Victor take the last few steps of his life. Victor resembled a zombie stumbling down the hall. Sheer adrenaline keeping him alive, but even that would only last for so long. Coleman smiled as he watched Victor try to save himself.

Sarah saw him first. She screamed before thinking it was another prank. She walked up to her wide-eyed classmate, his hands clutching the bloody blade lodged into his chest.

"Another joke, huh? It won't work this time. So cut it out!" she said.

Victor's bloody body fell forward in front of her and landed face down with a thump, forcing the sickle through his chest and out his back.

Sarah screamed, realizing it wasn't a joke. The other kids ran to her and saw Victor's body in disbelief, as blood pooled under him. The blade protruded through his back as a calling card from the Mangler.

Jake made his way through the fourth-floor door just in time to see the kids huddled around Victor's dead body. Sarah, shaking and sobbing, and near shock, looked up and saw Jake and screamed again. Everyone looked up and saw a tall figure in the shadows blocking their only exit. More of the girls screamed before Jesse realized it was only Jake. The group breathed a sigh of relief.

Russell kneeled at Victor's side doing what he could to save him, but the more he tried, the more he sobbed in the helpless situation.

"What the hell are you kids doing!?" Jake walked closer to the group and saw the boy's dead body on the floor. He paused. "Shit. You kids get out of here," he said softly. Too many thoughts ran through his head—sadness, fear, doubt, guilt—but deep down, he knew nothing could have prevented this from happening. He finally snapped out of it. "GET THE HELL OUT OF HERE! NOW!!" he screamed. This time, they didn't hesitate. All, but Russell and Jesse, grabbed their purses and phones and ran down the hall, some crying, some screaming.

Their sounds of terror faded as they trampled down the stairs.

Brandon hid behind the door as the terrified teenagers ran by. He was scared now, more than ever, but he was too close now, he had to see.

"Come on, Russ! We gotta get out of here," Jesse pleaded. Russell looked down at his friend and teammate, trying to take in the moment. Blood covered his hands.

He cried.

Jesse grabbed his arm and lifted him to a standing position.

"Go. You boys need to get going now," Jake told them. "Did you hear me? I said NOW!" he yelled.

Russell looked at Jesse, confused, before both ran up the hall and into the dark stairwell.

The thunder and lightning, in the distance earlier, now loomed over the town and hospital. Not every upper floor window was boarded up, allowing the lightning to cast its eerie flashes down the hallway. Jake stared at the dead body, shaking his head, anger sweeping over him. He had enough of the Mangler—no more visits, no more visions, no more secrets. He had to settle this now.

The music still blared from the stereo as Brandon carefully peered around the fourth-floor door. He saw Jake but was afraid to speak up, knowing he should have run to safety with the others.

Jake found a blanket from the party and used it to cover Victor's body. He walked over to the stereo and turned it off, sending the floor into a deafening silence. He knew this would all end now. He felt responsible for the boy's death and could not keep the secret any longer.

An unmistakable feeling hit him again, one he knew very well—Coleman was near. Jake turned to find Coleman standing not more than twenty feet from him. This was the closest they had ever been to each other, but this time, it was not just Coleman, it was the Mangler.

This time, he was not a ghost.

This time, he was real.

He smiled at Jake.

Jake tried to hide his fear and use the power he had used before to make him disappear. "That won't work now, old man," Coleman said. "I have been released and tasted blood again. I can smell my victims, their sweet smell of fear." He laughed, never taking his eyes off Jake.

Jake had never heard him speak, which proved to him that Coleman was indeed alive and living in the real world. Jake stayed calm and studied the killer, and wondered how much power he had in the living world.

Brandon stood in the shadows, looking on in awe and amazement.

Was he really seeing the ghost of the Mangler? He wanted to run down the stairs, but his fear froze him like a statue. He felt the warm fluid running down his leg as he lost control of his body. Brandon shook so much his vision became blurry. He was close to going into shock.

"You don't scare me," Jake told Coleman. "Dead or alive, you don't scare me." Jake calmly put a cigar in his mouth, pulled out a match and lit it, trying to hide his shaking hand.

Coleman was changing in front of his eyes.

41

Maybe, just maybe, whatever power I have is working, Jake thought.

But Coleman didn't disappear into a mist like before. He grew stronger. Jake realized Coleman was now holding a sickle and a chain.

Jake knew this confrontation would be their last. Coleman had just killed an innocent boy and that gave him the power to come back to this world and murder again. The power he had over the serial killer, one he didn't understand, he needed now. The only thing he had done since he began coming up here was standing his ground and looking right into the eyes of the murderer, never wavering. This always worked, and kept Coleman in the spirit world.

Since the day in ICU, when Coleman pointed at him just before he died, the two were connected. Now, it came down to this, and he had no idea how to stop it.

Jake puffed on his cigar, the fiery red tip burned and crackled. The smoke swirled and drifted in circles in front of him as he exhaled.

If this bastard is real now, I should be able to hurt him.

Brandon didn't know what to do. He couldn't move. Peeking through the crack in the door, he felt as if he was standing right between the monster and the man. But they had no idea he was there, as long as he stayed in the dark.

Jake reached for his crowbar on the table.

"Go ahead, take it," Coleman told him. "It won't do you any good. Your power over me is gone." Coleman stepped forward raising the sickle and chain. The crowbar slipped through his fingers and clanked on the cement floor. Coleman moved in with the sickle raised, about to strike down in his trademark murdering style.

Jake closed his eyes.

This was the end.

Brandon watched, mouth wide open, and began to cry.

Behind his closed eyes, Jake waited to be struck down, but nothing happened. He opened his eyes, the cigar fell from his mouth.

Coleman was gone.

Jake looked around, not knowing if Coleman had disappeared into a mist as before or if he had escaped.

He heard a noise behind him in the stairwell and turned quickly. He bent and picked up his crowbar and walked cautiously towards the door, raising the piece of steel as he did. He heard Brandon crying just inside the doorway. "What the hell are you doing here?" Jake asked as he lowered his weapon. "I told you boys, to get out of here. I'm not gonna say it again!" Jake was mad now. Damn kids.

"I'm by myself," Brandon said.

"Here, take this flashlight and get out of here," Jake said, "and don't come back, ever again."

Just as Brandon took the light, he glanced over Jake's shoulder and saw the Mangler looming a few feet behind him. Brandon's eyes widened and tried to point over Jake's shoulder, but his fear kept him from raising his arm. The flashlight in his hand felt like it weighed a hundred pounds. Jake saw the look in Brandon's eyes and knew what was waiting for him.

Brandon turned and ran down the stairs with the erratic beam of light leading the way.

Jake reached out and closed the old metal door. He was now alone with Coleman. He turned to face his fate.

Coleman, for the first time, looked more threatening to Jake, more like the infamous Mangler—a name he refused to acknowledge in his presence, but now, he could no longer deny they were one in the same. The Mangler stood with a shiny new sickle in one hand, and a brand new chain in the other. He was no longer a misty apparition as he had been before. He had transformed into the *real* world after killing Victor.

Jake, out of habit, reached for his cigar, but the one he had just lit, was gone. He smiled.

"You know what I just figured out?" The Mangler stood silently listening to Jake. "I don't know why, never have, but I still have power over you, because if I die, you die forever."

The Mangler raised the sickle again, lifted the chain and took a step towards Jake.

"You're not leaving here without me, old friend," Jake said, running towards Coleman, with the crowbar raised high. The Mangler's eyes locked on his next victim . . . Jake.

Brandon had made it down to the second floor when he heard a long groan from above. The sound made him stop and grab the railing. He looked up into the darkness, knowing it was Jake. He let go of rail and ran faster than he had ever run before, certain he was running for his life.

Authorities found Jake's body hanging from the old piping on Floor Four. He, like the contract worker, was hung by a chain. Jake's throat was slit, with the sickle lodged in his chest, in true Mangler fashion.

After a long investigation, the case was unsolved and considered a homicide. Everyone at the party that night became a suspect, but after the interviews, no leads were found.

Brandon *was* interviewed after he came forward about being there, but no one knew that he saw David Henry Coleman. Being young and scared, he never told the whole story. He was afraid the Mangler would come after him since he knew the truth and was the last one to see him.

He knew who murdered Jake.

3

NEW BEGINNINGS

*O*ne Year Later...

"We are standing just outside the site of the soon-to-be-demolished, Saint Vincent Hospital," the female news reporter from Channel 13 said. "Almost a year to the date since the double-murder of Jake Felder and Victor Ramirez, the old hospital has been secured and boarded up for safety concerns, and for the ongoing murder investigation. Investigators tell us, over that period of time, all possible evidence has been taken from this location." The reporter talked over old footage being shown to viewers. "Despite protests from some members in the community, the sixty-two-year-old hospital will be demolished tomorrow. Rumors continue to persist that the ghost of serial killer, David Henry Coleman, known as the Mangler, still haunts the building. Even a full year after the last murders, some say the ghost of Coleman is responsible." The reporter paused as a picture of Coleman was shown to the viewers. "But after the demolition tomorrow, we may never know the truth. On location in Baytown, this is Cynthia Hanson reporting for Channel 13."

The demolition took place the next day. News stations, reporters, citizens and all the kids who were at the party that rainy night, watched from behind the safety barricades. Brandon also watched.

The hospital went down in a heap of concrete, steel, and rubble, without a problem. Most curious onlookers left after it met its fate, but Brandon and a few others watched as crews moved in to remove some of the debris. Brandon found many things to keep his mind off what he saw that night, but he had to see the old building go down for himself.

A large machine with a front-end loader was slowly plowing towards a pile of debris when a ground worker signaled for him to stop. "Stop! Stop!" The worker bent down and began sifting through a small pile of rubble. "What the hell?" he said to himself. "No way."

The big piece of machinery suddenly stopping, and the yelling of the worker got Brandon's attention. He watched as the worker moved a couple of pieces of metal and then lifted a thick, shiny silver chain.

Brandon looked on in horror as he realized what it was. He shouted out loud, to no one in particular. "LOOK!" His eyes wide, he pointed at the worker.

"This looks brand new, no way," the worker said. Then he reached down and lifted the other piece he had found, a sickle. It shined like new, as did the chain. "What the hell is going on? How did this get here?"

Brandon looked on, as the construction worker lifted the sickle and chain high over his head and shook his arms violently.

"Look. I'm the Mangler!" the worker said, as he laughed aloud.

The sunlight reflected off the sickle's blade and shined right into Brandon's horrified eyes. The worker turned his head and looked right at Brandon, but Brandon no longer saw the construction worker holding his tools of murder . . . he saw the Mangler.

That night, Brandon stared at the ceiling in his bed, unable to sleep. With the hospital now gone, he was avoiding the latest text messages from Doug and Kyle, not wanting to share what he saw the night of the murders. In deep thought, he tried to understand his visions of the Mangler, when a knock came at his window.

It has to be them, he thought.

He got out of bed and walked in the dark room toward the knocking. The flash of lightning briefly lit the room as he stood in front of the window. Brandon slowly lifted one of the blinds, expecting to see Doug and Kyle. Another flash of lightning hit, but he couldn't see anyone.

Maybe it was the wind.

He walked away but stopped in the middle of the room when he heard the unmistakable sound of something slowly scratching on the glass. A chill came over him.

Lightning flashed again.

The slow and deliberate scratching left him with two choices—run to his parent's room, or see who or what was out there.

Despite everything that had happened, Brandon was still a curious kid. He turned and walked to the window.

Thunder shook the room, and as the rain came down in sheets, the scratching stopped. Brandon took a deep breath, grabbed the string, ready to pull up the blinds. It was time to face what was out there.

He pulled on the string, lifting the blinds, lightning flashed again. No one was there.

Then, suddenly…

Jake appeared, the palms of his hands slammed flat against the window. Startled, Brandon stepped back. Jake put his face, twisted with despair, to the window as rain poured down.

Brandon trembled.

"Run boy, run," Jake pleaded. "Run!"

Tears filled Brandon's eyes, sorrow setting in. In a flash, a chain flew over Jake's head and around his neck, wrapping tightly as Jake grabbed at it. Something more powerful than any living man, slung him backward. Jake hit the muddy grass, and in his place stood, David Henry Coleman. With his right hand, he lifted the chain, bringing Jake off the ground, his body shaking as he gasped for air. The Mangler held a sickle in his left hand and stared at the scared kid on the other side of the window.

Thunder and lightning struck again.

"You can't escape me. Anyone who sees me must die," the Mangler said, coldly. He dropped Jake's dead body, landing in the mud with a splash. "I'll be coming for you," he told Brandon, who was now crying.

The Mangler burned one last evil look into Brandon's eyes just before he turned and walked towards the woods with Jake's lifeless body dragged by the long chain.

Afraid to move, Brandon watched, knowing Jake's ghost tried to warn him one more time. He turned to run from his room and as he took his first step, he looked up and saw the Mangler's bloody sickle lodged in his bedroom door. Trapped in his room, and afraid to look back to the window, he glanced at the sickle before running to the door. Without looking up, he tried to turn the knob, but in his scared and panicked state, he couldn't get it to turn. He closed his eyes and tried to will the fear from his mind. He stood there a few seconds more, as thunder shook the house again.

Taking a deep breath, he tried the door once again, the knob turned easily. With his eyes closed, he let out a short sigh-of-relief and opened the door. The impaled sickle swung with the door, and after a quick look into the hall, he ran to his parent's room.

He burst into their room and saw his parent's empty bed. Panic set in again as he caught something out of the corner of his eye.

Standing completely still, and slowly turning his head, Brandon looked to his left. Something loomed in the dark shadow of the room. Lightning flashed through the window and to his horror, he saw his parents hanging from the ceiling. Their lifeless bodies slowly swinging from the chains wrapped around their necks.

Brandon's vision went black and he passed out, dropping to the floor.

Brandon's parents woke up to find their son on the floor, passed out. "I don't remember anything," Brandon told them. "I must have had a bad dream or something," he said.

Brandon's mother didn't hide her concern. She sat on his bed, next to her son, holding his hand. Brandon's father stood over them, looking at his son, silently contemplating what they should do next.

Considering everything over the last year, from the murder at the hospital to the recent demolition of the cursed building, his father knew Brandon had gone through a tremendous ordeal. And while they were upset with him for being there the night of the murders, they were very thankful their son was still alive.

"Do you remember anything from your dream?" his father asked. "Did it have to do with this thing at the hospital?"

His mother gave his father an angry look. She felt it was best if they put that behind them and concentrated on moving forward with their lives.

Brandon remembered everything from the dream if that's what it was, and he remembered everything from a year ago at the hospital. He never told anyone about that night on the fourth floor, and he wasn't going to start now. To the police, and everyone involved in the investigation, he was just one of the kids in the wrong place at the wrong time.

He glanced up at his bedroom door, looking for the sickle, but it was gone. Everything about the night before pointed to it being a dream or vision, but he knew the Mangler was coming for him.

"No, it wasn't about the hospital. I think I just got scared by the weather," Brandon told his dad. "I'm okay," he said, turning to his mom.

Her concern still showed on her face, but she smiled at him as she leaned in to kiss his cheek. "Get some rest, dear. I'll check on you later."

"You sure, you're all right?" his father asked.

Brandon nodded and smiled at his father, who wasn't so sure, but he let him be for the time being and left the room with his wife.

Brandon's parents, Daniel and Alicia, were concerned, as any parent would be if their child had gone through an experience as their son had. Brandon was fine physically, but the emotional scars left behind are what worried them the most.

Brandon got up and walked to the door. He slowly pushed it closed and looked up to where the sickle was the night before. He reached up and felt for a split in the wood. He ran his fingers back and forth over the smooth surface, finding no trace of a gash.

Somewhat relieved, he walked to the window and raised the blinds. The sun shined bright through the window, much different from the previous night. He looked outside for any trace of the Mangler's footprints in the mud or any proof of Jake's body being dragged across the yard. Everything looked normal.

As he backed away, he looked at the windowpane and paused when he saw something on the glass. He stepped to the window, stopped and saw Jake's smudged handprints on the glass. His eyes grew wide and he reached to touch the glass. To his shock, the handprints were on the *inside,* and small pieces of dried mud fell to the floor as he touched them. Brandon pulled back his shaking hand, quickly lowered the blinds, jumped back in bed, and cowered under the covers.

It wasn't finished with him, but he couldn't tell a soul. He felt afraid and alone.

Over time, most people put the murders and the old hospital behind them and went about their daily lives. Although the murderer had not been found, it was old news, but for Brandon, everything he had experienced was as if it just happened. No one knew the Mangler was still out there searching and hunting for more victims, with him being next. No one knew the ghost of David Henry Coleman grabbed a new energy by killing Victor and Jake and planned to kill again. The only ones who had any idea there was more to the story, were his *friends*, Doug and Kyle.

Doug and Kyle were the ones who took him to the old hospital. They showed him how to get in, and if they didn't believe in the ghost before that night, they did now. For some time after the night of the party, they were almost relentless, especially Doug, in asking him about what he saw. He didn't like Doug and always denied seeing anything, and after a while, the questions slowly stopped. But with the hospital's demolition, and all the media coverage of the rumors of the Mangler, the boys found themselves gripped again by the unanswered questions.

As the hot summer weather began to break, and the temperatures turned cooler, he found himself riding his bike a lot more in the evening. And this is where he would run into his friends, and when the questions started again. Brandon continued to hold his ground, but they didn't believe him and this caused friction between them. If he thought it would help, he would just tell them everything, but that wasn't the solution.

Brandon rode his bike a couple blocks to the Quick Stop convenience store on the corner. A place he liked stopping at and picking up some snacks. Digging deep into his pocket, he discovered he had more money that he thought, so he threw a bag of Funyuns on the counter with his snacks. As he paid, he saw Doug pull up outside on his old Huffy bike.

Great, he thought.

Doug, recognizing Brandon's bike, waited for him outside.

"What's up, Doug?" Brandon said as he walked out the store.

"Nothing, just riding around. What are you doing?" Doug asked.

"The same, just picking up some stuff to take home."

"You been by the old hospital lately?" asked Doug.

"No. Why?"

"They're building something over there. I don't know what it is, but they're planning something." Doug said, looking at Brandon, waiting for his reaction.

Brandon took the cap off his Dr. Pepper and took a drink. He didn't mind making Doug wait for a response because he didn't like him, especially after everything that had happened.

As the cold sweet taste of the soda washed down his throat, he put the cap back on, twisting it tight before he spoke. "Maybe they'll build another one," he said.

"Another one, what? Doug quizzed. "Another hospital? Are you kidding? Doesn't that bother you?"

Doug had asked more questions in the last ten seconds than his parents did in an entire day.

"It doesn't bother me. Maybe it will make people forget anything ever happened there." Brandon shrugged, dropping his soda into his bag.

"You're crazy. But you know more than you're saying," Doug said, looking at Brandon distrustfully. "Building something there will bring it back." He laughed.

Brandon shrugged his shoulders and shook his head. "I don't know." He did his best to hide his true feelings and got on his bike.

"If this stuff about the Mangler and the hospital doesn't bother you, you're crazy or hiding something." Doug gave Brandon an angry look and rode away in the opposite direction.

Brandon watched him ride off, knowing Doug was right.

He rode his bike to the store intending to swing by Jake's house after. He had only been by there once in the last year and with this last vision of Jake, he needed to see the house—for old times, old memories, or maybe to connect with Jake's spirit—if that was even possible. With Doug telling him about the new construction on the old hospital land, he wanted to ride by there too.

No one lived in Jake's old house. Brandon heard that Jake's family cleared out his belongings after the reading of his *will*. Straddling his bike, he stared at the *For Sale* sign slowly swinging back and forth on its hooks. Grass grew tall along the chain-link fence and he could see a few weeds popping up near the porch. That was Jake's favorite spot to sit and watch people go by, and occasionally tell kids, at least the ones who knew him, the scary tales of the hospital and more.

He didn't know Jake all that well, and had only visited him at his house a couple of times, but he always felt comfortable there. Without Jake, the deserted house looked and felt completely different. Over the passing time, he could see the paint was chipping. The curtainless windows stared back at him. Against his better judgment, he got off the bike and dropped the kickstand onto the sidewalk.

The gate wasn't locked and made an awful creak when he pushed it open, looking at the front door. No one was around, but it felt like the whole world was watching and as he closed the gate behind him, his sense of security and comfort seemed to leave him. He didn't know why he wanted to get a closer look, but he needed to face any fears he still had about the house.

The wooden steps groaned under his feet as he made his way to the porch. He smiled when he saw Jake's old, rusted metal rocking chair. Written with crayons, across the seat of the chair, in faded colors, were the words: *gRAnDpAs ChAiR*. Obviously a tribute from Jake's youngest grandchildren. He couldn't help but smile again.

Brandon slowly moved in front of a window just behind the chair, and despite the dust, could see himself in the reflection. He moved closer, and with his hand, he wiped a spot clean and pressed his face to the glass. His eyes darted left and right, revealing nothing more than an empty house—a house once full of life—a life taken away by the Mangler.

Feeling a bit more comfortable, he jumped off the porch and made his way around the side of the house. Leaves crunched beneath his feet as he got closer to the backyard. Everything seemed so quiet around him, when suddenly, the neighbor's dog, just on the other side of the wooden fence, began barking and growling. Surprised, Brandon almost ran into the side of the house jumping away from the angry dog. The dog continued to bark loud until its owner whistled for it to stop.

Breathing a little easier, Brandon noticed how dark it was in the shadows between the houses, so he walked to the middle of the small backyard and stood in the sunlight. The sun's warmth felt good as he stood in the backyard for the first time. He looked at the back of the house and noticed the paint chipping there as well.

The wood-framed house sat on cement blocks as many of the older homes did in that neighborhood. Brandon noticed how dark it looked under the house and shifted his eyes to the back door secured by a padlock and a latch. He was too short to look into the back windows, but the door had a small window he might be able to look in.

The back porch was half the size of the front. The wooden door looked newer than the rest of the house, and the window on it was too small for anyone to climb through. To his disappointment, Brandon was a couple of inches too short to see in, but after a quick look around the yard, he saw a plastic milk crate. After moving it to the base of the door, he climbed up and looked inside the house through the little window. He saw the kitchen, with the stove still in place, and assorted paper and trash scattered on the dusty floor. A doorway to the front room was on the right, and on the left, a hallway leading to the rest of the house. Out of the corner of his eye, he thought he saw something move in the hallway, his eyes stayed fixed in that direction, but nothing more moved as he looked in. Just as he was about to climb off the crate, he saw a shadow at the end of the hall.

"Hey! What are you doing there?" A voice called out from behind.

Brandon froze, afraid to turn around, his eyes still locked on the hallway.

"Get away from there, boy!" the man said, his voice sounded familiar.

Brandon turned slowly to see who it was. He knew he recognized the voice when he saw who was standing there.

The man looked just like Jake.

Brandon, still standing on the crate, fell back against the door. He shook his head trying to clear his vision, unsure if he was looking at Jake.

"Who are you?" the man asked.

Bang! Bang! Bang!

The door rattled against Brandon's back. The banging coming from inside the house. Brandon felt trapped and gave the man a quick look before jumping off the crate and running off the porch. He turned the corner of the house and ran to his bike, never looking back.

Jake's twin brother, who Brandon did not know, was taking care of the house while it was being sold. He shook his head as he watched the scared boy run away.

"Damn kids!"

Jake's brother walked up the steps and to the door. He thought he had heard a knocking on the door too. After looking inside the house through the window and seeing nothing, he picked up the crate and tossed it off the side of the porch.

Scared and breathing heavy, Brandon rode his bike home as fast as he could. He had intended to ride by the old hospital, but now all he wanted to do was get home. He wasn't sure about who he saw, but he was sure Coleman had something to do with it.

Two days passed before Brandon decided to go outside. The incident at Jake's house scared him, but he made up his mind to fight back against his dead enemy. He hadn't heard from Doug or Kyle during that time, which was a relief. Kyle was Doug's friend, but was nothing like him—as a matter of fact, Brandon liked Kyle. He could see them turning into good friends if it wasn't for Doug's mental bullying. Kyle was his own person, but as Brandon had come to learn, Kyle was a prisoner in Doug's world.

Brandon rode his bike to the municipal library, next door to the old hospital. His newfound bravery willed him to find out as much as he could about the past, so he could defeat his nemesis.

Before going into the library, Brandon stopped by the old hospital site. He had wondered if Doug was telling the truth about the new construction. The empty piece of land looked a lot smaller without the hospital there, and true to Doug's word, most of the ground had been cleared, and piles of dirt stood in various spots on the outer edges of the property. A sign, propped up by wooden stakes, stated something about the new happenings, but it faced the opposite direction. He was sure it said...*COMING SOON*.

Thinking back to that unbelievable night, made him feel uneasy standing there. He didn't know how to feel about something new being built there, and he guessed it really didn't matter what it was as long as it didn't bring *it* back to haunt whoever worked there. One thing he did know . . . *it* would find him.

Brandon pushed his bike forward and headed for the library entrance.

He could hear a storm brewing in the distance coming from the north, reminding him of the night Jake and the Mangler appeared at his window.

In the library, he found out as much as he could about David Henry Coleman. Articles in magazines and newspapers reported the serial killing spree over the years, but he found most of the information online. He heard someone planned to make a movie, but he didn't have time to wait for that. He didn't really know what he expected to find out about Coleman, but if he could find something, maybe a weakness in the killer, he might have a chance.

One show ran on the BIO Channel and Brandon took notes, having to watch it when his parents weren't around, but a lot of what they covered, he had already found out in his own research. The more he learned about Coleman, the more confident he became about stopping him. Since that day at Jake's old house, nothing strange had happened, leaving him unsure when he would appear again.

The next day at school went well and Brandon felt like he was finally picking up Mrs. McChessney's teaching style in American History. He had done well on the last two tests and hoped to raise his grade by the end of the six-week period. The school was close enough that his parents trusted him to ride his bike. All things considered, he felt older. The house and his school were on the other side of town from the hospital and Jake's house—something he was grateful for. He didn't have a fear of either, but not seeing them every day helped him grow stronger against whatever the Mangler had planned next.

The sun beamed down as Brandon coasted the last few feet up his driveway to the front porch. He didn't notice at first, but stuck in the front door of the house was a sickle, just like the one Coleman used. The sickle, shiny and new, was about three-quarters of the way up the door—the black handle, suspended in the air.

Brandon let go of his bike without dropping the kickstand, and it fell with a rattling clunk to the ground. He stared in disbelief, mesmerized by the sight of the sickle. After a few seconds, he looked around the front porch for any other strange things left around, mainly, a set of chains.

With apprehension, he slowly walked to the front door, his eyes never leaving the sickle. Now standing only a couple of feet in front of the door, he looked up at the intimidating sight. Deciding what to do next, he took a quick glance around the front yard—his only comfort was the warmth of the sunlight.

A mother pushing a baby stroller, another sign of comfort, walked happily down the sidewalk, never noticing Brandon. He turned back to the door, and just as he made up his mind to grab the sickle and pull it from its perch in the door, he heard a thumping coming from inside the house. His hand froze, now only inches from the black handle. His eyes darted left and right, listening for more sounds with the scene reminded him of his visit to Jake's house.

Is the Mangler haunting me?

He tried to shake the thoughts from his head and reached out to dislodge the tool.

His body tensed as small rocks crashed against the front window and fell to the porch floor. Brandon quickly turned and saw Doug with some other boy he didn't recognize, poking their heads up from behind the hedges just in front of the house. They laughed and ran away. Brandon wanted to chase after them but thought better of it. He could hear their laughter and mocking chants about the Mangler.

He was alone again and turned back to the sickle. Just as he reached up to grab it, it fell and rattled to the porch floor, scaring him. He stepped back and grabbed the railing. Taking a deep breath, and determined to fight through his fear, he walked to the front door, looking at the rocks—a reminder that this was all a joke.

Not knowing what pounded against the door from inside, he picked up the tool. The handle felt good in his hand, surprising him. No longer afraid, he almost found a smile come across his face when he jokingly thought of using it to get back at Doug. He looked at the door and could not find the gash where the sickle was lodged. Uneasiness set in.

Brandon held the sickle against his chest when he heard the sound of a car coming up the street. Hoping it wasn't his parents, he glanced over his shoulder. The white station wagon belonged to a family a few houses up the street.

Looking down at the sickle, he decided to hide it with some of his old bicycle parts. As he walked around the house to the backyard, a brisk breeze blew across the yard, giving him a chill.

Brandon found an old copy of The Baytown Star on the coffee table a couple of days later. The headlines read: OLD ST. VINCENT HOSPITAL LAND PURCHASED. The article told of the coming business, Bay Coast Medical Center, and how long it might take to build it. The official groundbreaking would be the following week. All just a constant reminder of the past that wouldn't go away.

As far as his parents were concerned, the hospital's demolition was for the best. They hoped it would help Brandon get past that tragic night, and put it all behind him.

But as Brandon knew, he had experienced much more than just one night. His experience a year ago, and the things still happening now were enough to last a lifetime.

With Jake gone, there was no one to talk to, and surely no one who would understand, much less, take him seriously.

He thought of Jake every day and always felt a sense of guilt over his murder. If it hadn't been for him and the other kids that night, he may still be alive. Jake had it under control until everyone messed it up. In the back of his mind, he knew he would see Jake again in one form or another, but he knew he was pretty much on his own.

Brandon waited each day for the Mangler to strike again and finish the job, and although he knew a lot more about him, he still felt helpless.

Thursday after school, Brandon got home without any jokes or ridicule directed toward him. He took a glass from the cabinet, filled it at the sink, and looked out into the backyard at his pile of old bike parts, thinking of the hidden sickle. As he downed his second glass of water, he stopped mid-swallow and focused on the wall above his little junk pile. A long, rusty chain hung on the side of the storage room. His mind raced as he lowered the half-full glass to the counter.

Placing both hands on the counter, he leaned over, to get a better look.

That chain wasn't there yesterday.

His heart raced, puzzled at the mysterious chain. He stared at the pile of bicycle parts looking to find the sickle, but from that distance, he couldn't make out anything in the garbled mess. Now he noticed how quiet the house was, quiet and deserted. Goosebumps covered his skin, making him feel unsettled, with his mind telling him to leave, but he couldn't take his eyes off of the chain. He wanted to go outside and see if it was real but felt if he took his eyes off the chain, it would disappear.

Everything felt strange, the house, the chain hanging outside, and the feeling of being watched. He decided to go outside and across the yard to the hanging chain. As he opened the back door, the wind picked up, blowing leaves across the yard. He looked in both directions and stepped into the sunlight. The chain hung as if it was on display for everyone to see. It creeped out Brandon, and he was sure the Mangler put it there.

His mind played tricks on him as he decided whether or not to grab it. A rattling from inside the storage shed startled him, and he took a step back. The shed door opened, creaking to a stop and leaves crunched under his steps as he moved around to see who opened the door.

His father came around the corner, much to Brandon's relief, and he almost burst out in a laugh at his overreaction, and for letting his imagination get the best of him.

"Dad?"

"Hey, son, did I scare you?" his dad asked.

"No," he said, bravely. "Why are you home so early, dad?"

"My truck broke down this morning, so I got off early to get some things in case I need to tow it home," his dad told him, as he set a small tool box down near the chain. "I borrowed this chain from Mr. Herring, next door." His dad reached over and lifted it off the hook and draped it over his shoulder.

"Everything okay, son?"

He looked up at his dad and smiled. "I'm okay. I better go do my homework," he said, looking to get out of the awkward moment.

His dad looked at him, still not convinced.

"I'll be inside," Brandon said.

"I'm getting a ride to my truck. Will you be okay here alone?"

The word, *alone*, made Brandon stop and think. Normally, he was never afraid or worried about staying alone in the house, but this time, with his imagination running wild, he didn't care to go back in the house by himself. Not wanting to worry his dad, he said, "I'll be okay, Dad."

"Okay. Make sure to lock the doors until your mother gets home."

The chains rattled as he watched his dad walk around the corner of the house. He quickly went inside and locked the door behind him and walked to the front window and watched his dad throw the chain in the back of his friend's truck.

The truck pulled away, and suddenly the house felt darker.

4

WASHING DISHES

The groundbreaking of the new hospital was only one day away. Brandon hadn't given it much thought in the days before, but now with it looming, and with the newspaper running a big article about it, his thoughts went back to the past events and secrets he held inside.

The night before the ceremony, Brandon watched TV later than usual and dozed off a couple of times, making him hungry. He walked to the kitchen and opened the fridge door, revealing just one piece of his mom's homemade apple pie. He smiled as he pulled it out and set it on the table. He didn't want to be the one to eat the last piece, so he grabbed a knife and fork and began to cut it in half. He heard footsteps coming from down the hall and looked to see his mother walking towards him, smiling. He blushed, feeling he was caught in the act.

Her smile changed to a shocked expression as she called out to him. "Brandon, what are you doing?!" She wasn't looking at his face, only at the table below. She ran to him.

Brandon's smile turned grim, puzzled by her reaction. He looked down at the table, to the pie and knife, and to his own horror, there was no pie. He trembled when he saw the knife had cut his hand with blood flowing from the cut onto the table. He let go of the handle as his mother rushed over to him, throwing the knife to the floor.

He looked up at her, not understanding what just happened, as she began to cry.

"No, Brandon, no," she cried. "This isn't the answer, baby." She held him close, her hand tight over his bleeding cut.

Brandon was in shock, hoping to wake from a dream.

"Daniel! Get in here!" she yelled. "It'll be okay. It'll be okay."

Brandon looked down the hall to see his dad running toward them. Just before Brandon passed out in shock, and with his vision blurring, his dad's face turned to that of a smiling, David Henry Coleman.

The investigation into what happened required extra time. Brandon was kept in the hospital for the night and most of the next day.

The cut on his hand took eight stitches, but would heal, and Brandon felt fine. The bigger problem, a cruel but necessary one, was evaluating his mental state, to determine his risk for suicide.

His parents claimed it was an accident, but were inwardly concerned, and because of Brandon's past in dealing with the murders, doctors remained skeptical and wanted to keep a close eye on him.

The groundbreaking for the new hospital came and went with Brandon still in the small hospital across town. Missing it was fine by him, but being under *observation* was almost too much to take. He often tried to eavesdrop on the doctors' conversations to get some idea of what they were thinking. By the end of the next day, they released him to his parent's care.

His parents always smiled at him, even if he could see the worry on their faces. He was just as worried as they were but glad to be going home, with no memory of him cutting his hand. He did know that Coleman was tormenting him, and again, he found himself feeling alone, with no one to turn to.

In the week after being released from the hospital, Brandon's parents, as any would have, kept a close eye on him. During that week, Brandon thought a lot about Jake and his warnings. Some days his thinking was very clear, but on other days, as if he was controlled by his ever-changing emotions. The one thing bothering him the most after he cut his hand was seeing Coleman's face instead of his father's. He felt weak and vulnerable when he thought about that dark moment as if he was being drawn in, with no way to stop it.

Over time, Brandon's parents felt comfortable enough to let him go out on his bike and do most of the things he had always done, except his time allowed away was cut in half. Their concern was to be expected.

One day while out on his bike, he felt drawn to the old hospital grounds—a place his parents forbid him to go. He pulled to a stop across the street. A bulldozer rumbled across the dirt, black smoke rising from its exhaust. In the far corner, part of the constructed building was in place. Looking at the land and the ongoing construction, it was hard for him to imagine the old hospital ever being there. He knew better, but in the back of his mind, he thought he might find the Mangler staring at him in the crowd of construction workers. The thought gave him a chill.

He peddled down the sidewalk, his curiosity satisfied for the moment and rode up Memorial Drive, he thought back to the day when Doug stuck the sickle in his front door.

That still made him so angry, he wanted to get back at him in some way. That time would come sooner than he thought.

On Friday night, Brandon's parents planned to go out for their anniversary dinner, but because of the ongoing situation, he would have to stay with a babysitter. He was upset at them for not trusting him and treating him like a child, but at the same time, he didn't want to ruin their night out. His babysitter for the night was their neighbor, and mother's good friend, Susan Davis. Brandon liked her because she always made him his favorite, homemade peanut butter cookies.

They would rather him stay over at her house, and although he didn't argue with them about the babysitting, he protested about not being able to stay at home. They compromised and asked Susan if she didn't mind staying at their house. She agreed with no problem, and as usual, brought a plate full of homemade cookies.

"Thank you again for doing this, Susan," his mother told her, with a concerned look on her face.

"Everything will be fine, Alicia. You two go and enjoy your night," Susan reassured her, patting her on the shoulder.

Brandon's mother nodded and leaned down to kiss his forehead. "Be good for Mrs. Davis," she told him. "Be sure to call me if you need anything."

The sound of the car horn from the driveway broke the short silence.

"Well, I better go."

"Have fun," Susan said, closing and locking the door behind her.

Susan turned to Brandon. "I know you want to do your own thing here at home and I don't blame you. I made those cookies for you so feel free to have as many as you like, without getting sick of course." She smiled at him.

He smiled back. "Thank you, Mrs. Davis."

"I'll be here in the living room watching TV if you need anything," she told him.

Mrs. Davis was in her late forties, young by most standards, but for most kids Brandon's age, she was old.

Brandon went to the kitchen and peeled back the shrink-wrap and immediately stuffed one of the warm, fresh-baked cookies in his mouth.

Heaven.

With a mouth full of cookies, he poured himself a glass of milk. He grabbed a paper towel, wrapping two more cookies in it, and headed to his room.

Mrs. Davis exchanged smiles with him as he walked by.

This Friday night felt like any other night as he finished off his last cookie while playing his PS3. He was just killed for the twentieth time in his game and hit the pause button. He stood and stretched, then walked over to the window, hearing the sound of the TV from down the hall. The breeze had picked up outside with the tops of trees, visible in the glow of the streetlights, slowly swaying back and forth. Looking into the darkness outside, he had to admit, he was glad Mrs. Davis was there with him.

An hour had passed since he came to his room. He looked down at the scar on his hand—healing, but a reminder of something he would rather forget. He understood in some ways why his parents were acting so protective towards him. He truly could not remember cutting his hand or anything happening between then and when he woke up in the hospital—except for the clouded vision of Coleman running towards him. Other than that, he felt fine, and although he knew the Mangler's ghost was still out there, he wasn't afraid of facing him if it came down to it. If anything, he felt he owed it to Jake.

The sound of laughter coming from the living room television broke him from his thoughts. Looking down at his own TV, he read the words on his video game, *You're Dead ... Game Over!* He needed a break and decided to grab another cookie from the kitchen.

The end of the hall opened up to the living room where he expected to find Mrs. Davis sitting on the couch. She wasn't there, but her reading glasses sat on top of her paperback novel. The volume on the TV was loud, but he paid it no mind and walked to the kitchen. Entering, he heard water running and saw Mrs. Davis standing at the sink with her back to him, washing dishes.

"Mrs. Davis, is it okay if I get another cookie?" he asked.

She didn't respond, and the upper half of her body slumped over the sink, her arms dangling to her side. Brandon's hand froze as he reached for a cookie, staring at her. Something was wrong.

"Mrs. Davis?"

Her knees buckled and her face plunged into the water-filled sink.

Brandon took a step back and looked around the kitchen, but nothing else seemed out of place. Not knowing if he was dreaming or delusional, he stepped towards Mrs. Davis. Her head began bobbing up and down, splashing the soapy water over the edge and down the cabinet doors.

Brandon watched in disbelief as the white soapy water began turning pink, and in seconds, a dark shade of red.

Her head rose higher and splashed down violently into the blood-filled water. Her arms still dangled and her legs, slightly bent at the knees, went limp—her body being held up by some unseen force. Brandon's eyes grew wider, as a tall, dark figure appeared behind her. It held her by a chain, tightly wrapped around her neck, and continued to slam her face down as blood spilled over the edge of the sink, running down to the floor. The all-too-familiar feeling of shock and helplessness held Brandon in place. He knew who this murderer was.

The Mangler, dressed in black, looked over his shoulder, staring back at Brandon. Laughter followed his evil grin and he lifted her with the chain, her feet leaving the floor. He spun her body around and Brandon immediately saw the source of the blood. Her eyes were gone, as blood poured from the dark hollowed-out holes in her skull.

Brandon finally snapped out of it and ran through the kitchen doorway to the living room, desperately seeking the safety outside the front door. He tried to open the door.

Locked!

He turned the deadbolt and unlocked the door, never looking back as he opened the door to escape.

The Mangler, holding his sickle and chain, waited for him just outside the door.

Brandon screamed.

5

A DARK ALLEY

*I*n the two weeks since the murder of Susan Davis and Brandon's disappearance, the trail left behind by the murderer had all the calling cards of the Mangler—the chain, the sickle and the nature of the violent murder. The police could not deny the almost perfect similarities, but they knew Coleman had been dead for years and assumed, like the murders at the hospital a little over a year earlier, this was the work of a copycat killer. While they searched for a suspect, their general suspicion was, the same person responsible for the hospital murders, abducted Brandon.

For Brandon's parents, his sudden disappearance left them grieving and worried with uncertainty. And like it or not, their son, even at his age, was once again involved in the investigator's search for the murderer. They knew their son did not murder Susan. Their priority was to find him and get him home safe and they made every attempt through the media, newspapers, and word of mouth to spread the word about their missing son. They pleaded to the killer on the news, to return their young son. In the two weeks since he disappeared, there were no clues or tips in solving the mystery.

The town was once again on edge with the possibility of another serial killer roaming their streets. Halloween was only a couple of days away and it was almost a certainty that most parents would keep their little ones at home and law enforcement discouraged trick-or-treating. Even teenagers seemed reluctant to embrace the dark holiday, with very few parties planned. Fear took over and most people took care of their errands by the light of day. It just felt safer that way.

Halloween night saw beefed-up police patrols combing the neighborhoods. And despite the overall sense of fear, there were quite a few trick-or-treaters out—mostly older kids and teenagers. The city hosted a party at the community building for younger kids and their parents, but rumors of a big high school party in one of the older neighborhoods made its rounds. A patrol car cruised the neighborhood as a precaution.

Doug talked Kyle into sneaking out with him to crash the senior party, but at the last second, Kyle changed his mind. His parents had a tight leash on him since Brandon's disappearance. Doug called him a wimp and turned his attention to his new friend, Cliff, who was with him when they pulled the prank on Brandon. Doug easily influenced Cliff, partly because he was just like him—unafraid and mean-spirited.

They both slipped out of their houses and made their way to the party. Luckily for them, the party was in their neighborhood, only two blocks away.

Even with Cliff going along with Doug, he was still a little worried about all the rumors of a killer. Desperate to make a friend in Doug, he kept his reservations to himself.

"How far away is the party?" he asked Doug.

"It's just up the road and around the corner. Not too far. Why? Are you scared?" he asked laughing.

"No. I just don't want my parents to catch me."

"Don't worry, we won't stay long if it's a lame party, or if those big bad seniors act like assholes," Doug told him. "Hear it?"

"Hear what?"

"The music."

A short distance away, rock music thumped in the air.

"Sounds like it's already started," Doug smiled and slapped Cliff on the shoulder.

The party was just up the block and around the corner. Doug stopped near an alley.

"Let's cut through here. We can get there quicker this way," suggested Doug.

Cliff looked down the shortcut. A crooked, old street light hanging halfway down the dark alley provided the only light. Overgrown bushes and tree limbs from the backyards reached over the fences, giving the alley an ominous look. It was a shorter route, but Cliff did not like the idea of going that way.

Doug started up the alley and stopped when Cliff didn't follow.

"Don't tell me you're gonna wimp out too?"

Trying his best to hide his fear, Cliff walked slowly towards Doug.

"It won't take long. I can hold your hand if you want?" he told Cliff, offering his hand, laughing.

Cliff slapped his hand away and sneered at Doug, his pride taking a hit.

They walked up the alley until they emerged from the shadows into the lighted area below the old street lamp. The light immediately gave them comfort, and a dog barking in one of the backyards gave the moment a sense of normalcy. The light only covered a small portion of the alley, and after a brief pause, they continued.

From the darkness at the other end of the alley, someone walked towards them. The sound of dried leaves crunched under the stranger's steps. The boys stopped, not saying a word, and noticed the dog had stopped barking. Everything went silent, except for the footsteps coming their way. They waited, but no one emerged and they looked at each other, no longer able to hide their fear.

Doug turned and spoke, "Who's there?" his voice cracking a bit.

No answer.

"It's some kind of Halloween joke," he told Cliff.

Chains rattled in the dark. Their fear grew. As hard as they tried, they could not see who or what made the sounds in the darkness. A six-foot length of chain flew from the blackness and crashed loudly at their feet.

Cliff didn't wait to see who threw it, and ran back the way they had come from. Doug turned quickly to watch him run from the light to the darkness, then turned to look at the chain lying in the dirt. He wanted to be brave and call out the pranksters, but he was scared and had a feeling this was not a joke.

From behind him, down the alley, Cliff screamed. Doug was almost in tears when he turned and saw Cliff, suspended in the air and moving towards him. His body, wrapped in chains, stopped just as it reached the light. The chains were wrapped around his chest and neck and covered his mouth. Something dark held Cliff in the air, his eyes wide with fear.

With nowhere to run, Doug had no idea what to do. He looked at Cliff hanging helplessly. The sound of the chains rattled behind Doug. He turned his back on Cliff to see who was behind him.

Brandon stood there, hanging the chain over his shoulders. A sudden feeling of relief came over Doug, seeing his classmate, but he didn't approach him. There was something about Brandon that told him to stay back. He looked different, not the usual happy, gullible kid he used to pick on. Even in the dimly lit alley, he could see Brandon's angry and menacing stare.

"Brandon? Is that you? What's going on?" Doug asked. He took the smallest of steps in Brandon's direction. And could still hear Cliff struggling with whatever was holding him.

"Remember me?" Brandon asked. The voice sounded nothing like his. "I'm back."

"What do you mean? You know me, it's Doug."

Brandon walked towards him, a sickle in his right hand. "Yes, you remember me well. You saw me at the old hospital."

Doug was confused. The person standing in front of him was Brandon, but the voice came from a deeper and darker place. "Brandon, it's me." Doug looked over his shoulder. Cliff, eyes still wide, was shaking his head, trying to warn Doug.

Brandon, dressed in black and only two short steps away, lowered his head. Doug's eyes focused on Brandon's right hand, and the sickle tightly wrapped in it.

"Anyone who sees The Mangler must die," Brandon told him. "You must die." He raised his head and his coal-black eyes met Doug's.

Doug stepped back. "I... I... didn't see anything."

Brandon smiled and raised the sickle high. Doug took another step back and bumped into a dangling chain. Not wanting to take his eyes off Brandon, he had no choice but to look up. Above him hung Cliff's dead, limp body, his neck bent—eyes still wide, but now in a dead stare. The chain was pulled so tight it crushed his neck completely. Blood dripped from his mouth.

Suddenly, Cliff's body was thrown to the side, the Mangler, eyes full of evil and death, stared down at him.

"Wait. You're dead, you're supposed to be dead," Doug mumbled. He dropped to his knees and he lost control of his body. Urine flowed down his legs. His body convulsed in fear.

Brandon admired the way Coleman took control and put the fear of death in anyone who saw him. His mentoring was paying off now.

"Kill him!" Coleman shouted. "Kill him."

Brandon looked at Doug and raised the sickle higher.

Coleman smiled.

Doug looked up at Brandon's black eyes and his blank stare. "Please. Please don't do this," he cried. His tears flowed, and just then, he saw a difference in Brandon's eyes. The blackness flickered and suddenly, he didn't seem as evil—a glimmer of hope.

Brandon's hand dropped. His grip on the sickle loosened.

"Kill the little maggot!" Coleman screamed. He lifted Doug by the collar and thrust him forward, in perfect position for the execution.

Brandon shook his head, as tears filled his eyes. Coleman's influence was losing its grip on him—his mentoring and power over the last two weeks, slowly fading.

"Do it or you will die too," Coleman said calmly.

Brandon looked up past Doug, and into the eyes of his supernatural mentor. His eyes were hypnotizing to Brandon. Coleman's influence grew strong again.

"Kill the little punk!" Coleman commanded.

Brandon's eyes went black again. Doug shook his head, slobber bubbled from his mouth and down his jaw. Coleman set him down for the execution.

Brandon raised the sickle one more time.

Doug closed his eyes.

Coleman smiled again.

Brandon yelled and charged forward. Just as he brought the sickle down, he pushed Doug aside. The sickle came forward, its point aimed perfectly at Coleman's chest.

"NOOOOOO!" Coleman screamed.

As the blade swung down and into the Mangler's chest, his body burst into a bright light, before fading and disappearing completely.

Brandon fell forward not expecting to swing the blade into a lifeless, disappearing figure. He tripped over Doug and fell to the alley's dirt road, the sickle falling from his hand. The chains rattled around him.

Doug looked up from his crouched position, not believing what just happened, not believing he was still alive. He rose and watched Brandon as he pulled off the chains and slung them on the ground. He turned to face Doug.

Doug slowly crawled away from him. He could see Brandon's eyes were no longer black, but he still feared him.

Brandon tried to shake out of his confused state. His mind tried to take in everything that had happened over the last two weeks—of him being taken by Coleman into some supernatural world. He tried to remember how he twisted his mind to kill Doug.

He didn't understand any of it and now had helped to kill another kid.

He looked over at Cliff's body and shook his head in regret.

Doug stood and looked at the twisted, dead body of his friend wrapped in chains. He was confused, shocked, and scared, and didn't know what to do.

Brandon, his head beginning to clear, picked up the sickle and turned towards Doug. He reached down to lift the chains.

"No. Please don't do it. I won't say anything." Doug said, wanting to run, but afraid to leave the safety of the light and into the darkness.

The chains rattled as Brandon put them over his shoulder. His emotions ran wild, enjoying the fear in Doug's eyes. He had always wanted to get him back and scare him, but he didn't want to kill him.

"I'm really messed up," he whispered to himself.

"What?" Doug asked softly, still cautious.

"I said, get out of here." Brandon raised the sickle. "Get out of here!"

Doug nodded, eyes wide, and ran down the dark alley in the other direction.

The dog barked again. Faintly, in the distance, Brandon heard the music and laughter from the party. He felt he was safe again, for the moment, safe from The Mangler. But the dead body of the boy lying in the alley was real. He knelt by his side as his vision blurred, and passed out.

Doug wanted to run home but ran to the party to get help first. Afraid and not wanting to be alone, he finally convinced the kids at the party to go to the alley. At first, his panicked and frightened face drew laughter from the teenagers, but it was only when Doug began to cry, did they take him seriously.

When the teenagers, all dressed in different costumes, from Leatherface to Batman, and ironically, one in a mock-up of the Mangler, made it down the alley, only Brandon remained, still passed out. There was no sign of blood, no sickle, and no chains, and most importantly, there was no Cliff. Doug looked around in disbelief, desperately searching for some sign of the murder, and the Mangler.

Jason, Frankenstein, and Michael Myers knelt down to help Brandon and called 911. The others looked around the alley from one end to the other and only found a dead rat in the garbage and trash. They turned to Doug for answers, but he had none, now more afraid than ever. He couldn't say it, but he knew the Mangler was still out there.

6

OLD FRIENDS

Eleven months had passed since they found Brandon in the alley that Halloween night. During that time, many questions were left unanswered. The investigation and search for Cliff Elkins turned up nothing, but continued despite Doug's claims of seeing him murdered that night. With no one to back up his story, investigators and family members kept the door open, hoping he would be found. But after a year, only family members continued the exhaustive search.

During that time, Doug never wavered in his account of what happened. He told anyone who would listen about Brandon trying to kill him and of Cliff being murdered. Investigators questioned Brandon in every way possible, from every angle possible about his whereabouts during the two weeks he was missing. He claimed only to remember being taken by a man who never showed his face. He didn't remember anything else about those two weeks or about that night in the alley. With no evidence and nothing else to go on, doctors and authorities released Brandon to his parents and put him under a rigorous schedule of mental evaluation and therapy.

Doug felt alone, betrayed and grew worse mentally, slowly pulling away from his parents and the world around him. He began having nightmares of that night, with a vision of the Mangler returning to kill him. After six months of visits with a psychologist, he wasn't getting better, regressing further and becoming more frightened. He knew he wasn't crazy, and felt everything he had experienced, was very real.

He and Brandon were not allowed to communicate unless it was in a controlled, monitored setting. This never worked, as Brandon continually told Doug he didn't remember anything. Frustrated by the same old story, Doug refused to continue the sessions. Instead, he sought out Brandon in other ways, without doctors hanging over their shoulders and listening to every word. Brandon knew the truth, but he never gave Doug a chance to confront him.

While Brandon's mental health seemed to improve, Doug got worse. His nightmares of the Mangler coming to get him scared him and drove him to a more reclusive and dangerous state of mind, with Brandon being the only one who could help him.

During this time, no more murders occurred, and authorities had not found a serial killer. For most outside of the ones affected, life was just about back to normal.

Growing increasingly frustrated, Doug gave up on convincing everyone about his side of things. He decided to wait for the right time to confront Brandon. Doug knew there was nothing wrong with him, but feeling separated and alone from the rest of the world drove him further into being a recluse. He knew his parents planned to get him more help, which meant new questions by new doctors.

His plan was to confront Brandon and try to shake him up, maybe get him to admit something, anything about that night, or even better, something about the Mangler. He knew he could catch him before he got home from school.

Doug no longer went to the same school as Brandon and skipped the day so he could surprise him after school. After making his plan, his anger multiplied each day he waited. He knew Brandon was lying, but he needed to know if the Mangler still controlled him. Doug suspected they were waiting for Halloween to start killing again, with him being the next victim. His head rang with the words: *Anyone who sees me must die!*

Doug waited down the street from Brandon's house. The sun shined bright in the blue sky and he stood in the shadow of a big oak tree near some bushes. He knew Brandon's route home by heart.

The yellow and black paint shined off the top of the bus as it turned the corner up the block. Doug moved from the tree and walked quickly to a row of shrubs and bushes along the sidewalk. The well-kept bushes stood six feet tall, giving him plenty of room to hide from Brandon.

The bus driver locked the air brakes and dust blew out in all directions from underneath the bus.

Doug peered through the thin branches and small leaves as four kids exited the bus. Brandon made his way down the steps carrying a backpack strapped over his shoulder. He was on a phone call as he crossed the street, and as the call ended, just as Doug had guessed, Brandon walked in his direction. Doug got in position, his heart raced faster, he wiped the sweat from his face.

When Brandon got within a few feet, Doug jumped from his hiding place and finally got to face his ex-friend, alone.

Brandon stopped in his tracks with a surprised look, bringing a smile to Doug's face.

"I finally get to talk to the guy who ruined my life," Doug told him.

Brandon remained silent, only looking at the agitated boy in front of him.

"I've been waiting a long time to talk to you." Doug stepped closer. Brandon didn't move, holding his ground. "Do you know, everyone thinks I'm crazy? The people at school, the doctors, and my parents, they all do. They think I'm making this all up," he told him, now standing only a couple of feet away.

Brandon looked around and finally spoke. "They thought I was crazy at first, too," Brandon told him, trying to say they were going through the same thing. He could see the angry look in Doug's eyes. "My memory started coming back and things got better."

"Your memory hasn't forgotten the truth. Why don't you just tell the truth?" Doug asked, his voice more agitated. "Why did you lie to the police?"

Doug had asked Brandon these questions before they went their separate ways, and as he did then, he denied remembering anything.

"I didn't lie. I was kidnapped and don't remember anything about the time I was gone."

"That's a lie!" Doug shouted.

"It's the truth." Brandon no longer felt intimidated by Doug as he did in the past and continued to stand his ground. He *was* telling the truth about not remembering a lot of it in one big blur. The one thing he would never tell was of him being Coleman's protégé. He did remember that, but didn't understand how he was able to enter the supernatural world and be brainwashed by the killer. He also remembered Coleman telling him he would spare his life if he took his place in the real world and continued his legacy. He knew Coleman would show up and tell him when it was time to kill again, but had not appeared to Brandon in the last eleven months.

"No, it's not. You're a liar. You have everybody fooled, but I know better!" Doug said.

An older woman raking leaves in her yard across the street, heard Doug's outburst and looked over at the boys.

Brandon shook his head, disagreeing.

"I know all about the Mangler killing anyone who sees him. We are the only ones who believe it. He has stalked me since last year." Doug's anger and frustration turned his face bright red.

Little did Doug know, Brandon was trying to protect him. He didn't know why, but for some reason, the Mangler had not killed Doug.

"I'm trying to forget about everything that happened at the hospital. I need to go," Brandon said, trying to walk around Doug.

Doug blocked his path, fists balled at his side. Brandon could see the tension in his face.

"I need you to tell everyone the truth and quit making them think I'm crazy. I know what I saw," Doug said.

"I have to go," Brandon said, once again trying to get past Doug.

Doug shoved him. The blow rocked Brandon's chest and pushed him back a couple of feet. He turned to run in the opposite direction, but Doug was too fast and grabbed him by the shoulders, dragging him down.

"Hey! You boys stop!" yelled the woman from across the street.

Bigger than Brandon, Doug easily overpowered him and hit him in the back with his fists, paying no mind to the woman who was now at the curb, ready to cross the street.

"You're gonna tell them the truth!" Doug yelled, saliva spewing from his mouth. He turned Brandon over and used his weight to hold him down.

Brandon, almost out of breath, raised his arms trying to throw him off.

Doug's tightly clenched fists pounded down on Brandon's chest and then on his face.

"Stop! I said!" The woman was almost to them.

Brandon blocked most of Doug's punches, but one finally slipped through, solidly landing on his nose. As his fist connected, blood exploded. The dark red liquid flowed immediately over Brandon's face. Doug paused, admiring his handy work and in seeing the blood, gave Doug another adrenaline rush and he raised his fist high.

Brandon threw his arms to the side.

"Come on! Hit me again," Brandon said, inviting Doug to do more damage. "You can't hurt me." Blood filled Brandon's mouth.

Doug paused again, surprised by Brandon's reaction. Breathing heavy, he brought his fist down.

The end of the metal rake crashed against the side of Doug's face, forcing him to draw in his fist and fall on his side.

"Leave him alone!" she shouted. "Quit hurting that boy."

The blow stunned Doug, and as he looked up at the woman, she prodded at him with the rake, forcing him off Brandon.

"Go on. Get out of here," she told him, holding the rake like a spear. "Are you okay?" she asked Brandon.

Brandon laughed louder, still lying on his back, blood running down the sides of his face.

Doug wanted one more shot at him. He wanted to hurt him real bad. He grabbed the end of the rake and pushed it, forcing the woman back. She lost her balance and fell backward into the street and her head slammed on the asphalt with a sickening thud.

A car horn blared as it swerved, barely missing her. The car behind it didn't have time to swerve and the driver slammed his brakes. The tires screeched to a stop only a couple of feet from hitting her.

The boys momentarily turned their attention to the injured woman.

Brandon refocused first and quickly turned and grabbed Doug, pulling him to the ground. And just as fast, he rose and straddled Doug before he had time to get up, pinning him with his knees.

Brandon reached for his back pocket and pulled out a small knife he carried for protection. He smiled as he took his time unfolding the blade. He didn't want to kill Doug, but now he wanted to hurt him bad.

Doug's heart raced, his breathing labored with the weight of Brandon on his chest. His bravado, all but taken now.

Brandon raised his hand above him, knife gripped tightly within it.

"Hey!" the man from the car yelled.

As if Coleman was guiding his hand, Brandon brought the small knife down and the two-inch blade sunk into Doug's upper chest, near his shoulder. Doug cried out in pain as Brandon pulled the blade out and raised it above him again.

The man had a running start and dove at Brandon, hitting him on his side, the momentum carrying them both over Doug and to the ground. The knife fell from

Brandon's hand and the man got to his knees and held Brandon on the ground.

Three more people joined in to help. A young woman dressed in hospital scrubs knelt over the woman in the street. A small amount of blood began to pool on the asphalt surface under her head. Another man came to Doug's aid, while the other helped subdue Brandon.

A police car arrived first, quickly followed by an ambulance and fire truck.

The knife wound in Doug's chest didn't penetrate deep enough to do any major damage. The doctor told Doug's parents the wound in his chest was in the best possible place it could have been. Doug would be okay.

The older woman wasn't as lucky. Despite the close call with the car, her head slamming into the road knocked her unconscious, giving her a severe concussion. Doctors kept her in ICU with hopes the swelling in her brain would go down enough to take the next step in her recovery.

The police took Brandon into custody and eventually into a juvenile detention center.

7

REUNION

The next three weeks were a blur for Brandon—a feeling he had grown accustomed to. His head hung low, chin to his chest, as the medication coursed through his body. A nurse pushed him down the hall for yet another round of mental observation and diagnosis. With his arms and legs strapped to the wheelchair, the ride seemed to take forever. The mild sedative given to him left him feeling weak and lifeless, but his mind remained clear and he always knew what was happening around him.

After three weeks in the detention center, things had not changed for Brandon. His mental state had deteriorated to the point that he was going to be transferred to a mental hospital for a more thorough evaluation.

The killings started again the first week in October with Gary Holloway murdered in his bed, while he slept. His throat was slit, and his chest impaled by a sickle. Police could not find a motive.

The shocking double-murder of Mark and Jean Ellis followed the next week. They were found by a family member, murdered in their barn, hung from the rafters with chains, their faces slashed beyond recognition—one of the

Mangler's trademarks. Mark and Jean had escaped Coleman's murder attempt years earlier.

Anyone who sees me must die.

Most alarming was the death of Doug Sellers, one week later. While recovering at home from the stab wound and the fight with Brandon, his mother found him in a sitting position with his back wedged in the far corner of his room. Even in death, his terror-filled eyes remained open and gazed upwards. The coroner ruled his death a heart attack, but his *unofficial* opinion of Doug's death, was shock, as if he was scared-to-death.

Oddly, in the short amount of time between his death and being discovered, the first stages of rigor mortis had set in, locking him into that sitting position in the dark corner of his room.

Because of the murders, some residents began questioning all logic and even entertained the thought of the Mangler being responsible. Reporters asked investigators about the Ellis family's connection to Coleman and the murder attempt years before. They answered with the standard, *no comment.*

Law enforcement, from local police to the FBI, knew they had a serious copycat on their hands. Not one of the investigators believed this was the work of Coleman or the ghost of the Mangler. They didn't deal in the supernatural. The facts were the facts—Coleman was dead. Around town, no one felt safe, and an after-dark curfew was finally issued for anyone under eighteen.

In his mental state, doctors did not allow Brandon access to the outside world and was not told of the recent killings, especially Doug's death. His parents did their best to help him pull out of his withdrawn state, but nothing seemed to work, and because he was not making progress, and on medical advice, the court decided to admit him to a secure mental hospital, better equipped for his condition.

The hidden, dirty truth was Brandon was trying to reconnect with Coleman ever since stabbing Doug and tasting blood for the first time. It was Coleman who mentored and took care of him, and that's how he saw him, not as a monster, but as a role model. But since that night in the alley, Coleman had not appeared in his dreams or within the strange supernatural world as he did before.

Brandon kept mental notes on everything around him, but he would not respond to his parents or the doctors for fear that Coleman would not approve.

Brandon believed his fight with Doug proved to Coleman, he was capable of doing *his* work. He regretted he had attacked his mentor last Halloween, and hoped the serial killer would forgive him. He had to keep up his charade with the doctors to allow him enough time to make contact with Coleman.

HALLOWEEN

The brand new, five-story, medical complex was a high-tech looking building with blue-tinted, mirrored glass. Just a bit smaller than the original hospital, this new business model brought three different levels of care all rolled into one. The first floor was administration, with floors two and three used as an ultra-modern assisted living area. The fourth floor was used as a hospice, and the newly opened fifth floor was a mental health facility, with the mantra: *'The Newest in Technology and Healthcare'*.

A smaller building sat adjacent to the main one as a registration hub for the three different services offered at the new facility. The complex looked nothing like the old hospital, and most people in town were excited about the jobs created by this shiny new business.

Brandon was admitted to the newly opened Bay Coast Mental Health Clinic, located within the shiny new medical complex. He didn't know he was being moved to the same location of the old hospital. His parents and doctors agreed there was no need to tell him for now.

Before being transported, Brandon was slightly sedated, just enough to make him drowsy. The meds would wear off by the time they got him in his room.

Brandon's parents waited with his doctor as the transport van arrived at the back of the hospital. After a kiss from his mother and a hug from his father, he was placed in a wheelchair and pushed into the back entrance near the rear elevator. The *Psych Ward* was on the fifth floor.

His parents, the doctor, and a nurse stepped into the elevator, and for safety and legal reasons, Brandon's wrists and ankles were strapped to the chair with wide leather cuffs.

The elevator had the newest in digital displays and surveillance monitors. Brandon's mother looked into the lobby as the elevator doors closed, with so many different thoughts buzzing through her head. Brandon was aware of his surroundings, and of being moved, but did not know the location.

The doctor leaned down. "Brandon, you are being taken to a different place, a place where you can get better care." He waited a moment but got no reaction. He stood up and nodded at Brandon's parents letting them know it was okay to speak to him.

His mother bent down. "Honey? Brandon? Are you feeling okay?"

Brandon nodded, but did not speak.

His mother patted his shoulder and stood up, noticing her husband's concerned expression.

The elevator passed the third floor as Brandon focused on the digital display. Then the fourth floor, and a moment later, the fifth-floor digit appeared on the screen, followed by the words—Psychiatric Care. The elevator came to a stop.

The doors did not open. Instead, the walls began to shake. The lights flickered and blinked off and on. The mild sedative given to Brandon earlier was wearing off.

His mother shrieked.

"Everything will be okay," the doctor said. "Probably just a temporary glitch."

The elevator continued shaking, banging and rattling. The sounds of metal clashing were followed by a sudden drop, and quick free-fall. Everyone let out a shocked..."Ohhh!"

The wheelchair rattled as Brandon's heart beat faster. He looked at his parents for reassurance, but only saw confusion in their eyes.

Without warning, everything went still and silent.

A red light flashed inside the elevator as an emergency buzzer sounded from within the panel.

The red digital display flashed, '4'...'4'...'4'. Brandon looked at it and a paralyzing fear set in. His only comfort was that he was not alone.

Ding.

A dark hallway greeted him as the elevator doors slowly parted. Brandon, who *had* wanted to reconnect with Coleman, now wanted nothing to do with him. Desperate to leave, he pulled against the straps, only they were no longer leather straps. He looked down and saw chains wrapped around his wrists and ankles. A dim light glowed at the end of the dark hallway.

Brandon turned his head to look behind him. His parents, the doctor, and the nurse, all stared straight ahead—their faces expressionless, bodies motionless. They looked towards the far end of the long hallway.

The wheelchair, now of decades past and made of wood, slowly rolled forward. Again, Brandon turned, no one was pushing him, the chair moved on its own, leaving the safe confines of the elevator and into the darkness. Lights flickered in the hallway, creating just enough light to illuminate his surroundings.

Brandon struggled against the chains as the lights went out completely. From a short distance, a light moved toward him before going out. The chair stopped moving, and the light flashed on again.

Brandon screamed as an old nurse, wearing an old hat and uniform from the 1940's appeared behind the light. The light only lit half of her smiling, shadowy face. Brandon leaned back as his heart pounded faster.

"Welcome to Floor Four," the nurse said with a big smile and the creepiest of looks in her eyes. Her red lipstick was smeared in a maniacal-looking pattern, most of it missing her lips completely. She stepped aside as the chair slowly moved forward. She stretched her arm out in front of him in the direction of the dark hall, inviting him in.

He tried to shake loose again as the doors to the rooms in the hall began to violently open and close. The sound of the doors slamming was so loud he thought his ears would burst. He turned and looked back at the elevator. Just as the door closed, he saw his parents, the doctor, and the nurse hanging by their necks. His eyes widened and he screamed.

The closing door sucked the last bit of light from the hallway.

The chair continued moving down the hall, doors still opening and closing. Paper and trash littered the floor with some floating and falling softly back to the floor. Sweat covered Brandon, and his wrists began to bleed from his struggle to free himself from the chains.

The hall doors slammed in unison, then opened. The hall went silent and the lights flickered. Hospice patients, long without hope of living much longer, appeared in each doorway. Brandon looked at the first one, an older man. The man pulled down his hospital gown showing his wide-open chest, revealing two damaged lungs, blackened by years and years of smoking, cancer staking its final claim.

"Got a cigarette?" he asked Brandon, with a smile.

Shocked, Brandon tried to turn his head away, but it was held to the back of the chair by another chain. He could not close his eyes, he had no control, and to his left stood an old woman holding something in her hands. As the chair moved closer, she stepped forward, holding her pumping heart.

"How's your heart, dear? Want to trade?" the woman asked, laughing hysterically. The heart beat faster, but where there should have been blood, black liquid oozed like thick syrup between her fingers.

He tried again to close his eyes, as the chair continued its journey down the hall, passing patient after patient—all of them dying. Each one there for their final days. He moved closer to the light at the end of the long hall.

Now to his right, another older man stood in his doorway looking straight ahead. He removed his sunglasses. His eyes had no pupils and glowed a solid white. He reached for Brandon as he tried to lean away, but the man's shaking hand grabbed his arm and squeezed. His other hand, fingers extending like claws, reached for Brandon's eyes.

"I got my eyes on you," the man said.

Brandon cried and tears filled his eyes. The chair rattled, and the man let go as it continued rolling forward.

The silhouette of a man stood in front of the frosted-glass door at the end of the hall, his features not yet visible. The chair stopped in front of the figure. The lights flickered, and through the flashes of light, his face became visible.

Jake.

His eyes were closed and his body limp.

This was too much for Brandon, and he struggled against his restraints, trying desperately to free himself and leave this evil place. His heart beat faster, his breathing heavy and labored, and began to bleed from the chains rubbing against his wrists and ankles.

Jake fell forward on top of him.

Brandon screamed again.

Jake's dead body slid and fell to the floor with a thud.

David Henry Coleman now stood in front of him, and even through the dim light, he could see his evil sneer. Brandon began to pass out.

"You can't hide that way," Coleman told him. He stepped forward and grabbed Brandon by his hair. "You betrayed me, and now you must die by my will and my rule."

Brandon looked at him, and strangely, was not afraid. He no longer wanted to be his protégé and wasn't worried about his fate. Somehow, he was at peace. A sense of calm came over him and he smiled.

"I see you didn't miss me at all," Coleman told him. "I came back to offer you a choice and to tell you how busy I've been." He reached over his shoulder and pulled out his sickle. "In the last three weeks, I have murdered again— each one, a connection from the past. The ones I planned to kill before. You're the only one left," he said, bringing the tip of the sickle to Brandon's chest.

Vomit filled Brandon's throat, no longer at ease. The cold metal of the steel blade gently slid up to his neck as Coleman walked around him. Brandon's heart pounded in his chest, sweat poured from his forehead, blood dripped from his wrists and ankles.

"Anyone who sees me must die," he told Brandon, "but I will give you a choice." He now stood behind him.

The wheelchair spun around quickly, the Mangler holding the handles.

Brandon's eyes widened seeing his parents standing in front of him. Strangely, they were smiling. He tried again to break free, desperately wanting to run to them and be saved, and ask them to forgive him.

"Do you want to live or die?" the Mangler asked.

The chains holding Brandon unraveled and dropped to the floor, landing in a clang of steel that echoed up and down the long hallway. He wanted to stand and run, but instead looked up at his parents, as they looked at him, smiling, oblivious to what was going on around them.

"Your choice . . . you or them," he told Brandon, as he walked and stood behind his parents.

Brandon now realized what he meant and he tried to clear his head.

He tried to reason with the killer. "But, my parents never saw you. Why do you want to kill them?"

"You know so little, but you think you know so much," the Mangler's tone, more menacing now. "I will not be killing them . . . you will," he said, as he walked between his parents, shoving them aside. He reached for Brandon, grabbing him by his shirt and pulling him up in a standing position.

Fear and doubt crept back into Brandon's eyes as he stared at the man in black, face-to-face.

"You or them!" Coleman yelled as he slammed the sickle into the wooden armrest of the wheelchair. He let go and the sickle stood on its own, impaled in the chair. He walked behind it.

Brandon didn't know what to do. He looked up at his parents, standing shoulder to shoulder, still smiling. He was more frightened than ever, but he knew it was time.

He reached out with his shaking, bloody hand and grabbed the sickle's handle tight.

The Mangler smiled.

Brandon paused, looked back at his parents, quickly pulled the blade from the armrest and faced them—their smiling faces still greeting him.

He quickly turned to the Mangler and swung the blade with all his might. He yelled, letting out his fears, frustrations, and anger all at once. He closed his eyes as he felt the blade drive into its chest.

He opened his eyes and his heart sank and a deep inner pain took over.

Fresh blood dripped of the blade, lodged in his mother's chest. He looked at her, then to his father, their eyes met his, no longer smiling. Their faces showed no anger or pain . . . only sadness.

Tears filled his eyes as he screamed at the top of his lungs, just as the Mangler's blade came down over him.

The sunny autumn day brought cooler air, as they moved Brandon from the transport van to the waiting wheelchair at the new hospital. His parents, his doctor, and a nurse all greeted him with smiles.

Now awake, but still drowsy from the sedative, Brandon could make out the people around him. His surroundings looked eerily familiar. He raised his head and looked around.

Afraid and confused, Brandon tugged against the straps as the dream he just had, came back to him.

The doctor patted him on the shoulder.

"You'll be fine," the doctor assured him. "Just relax, you'll be in your room soon."

Brandon wanted to get out of the chair, but the meds still had hold of him. The nurse pushed him through the lobby and to the elevator doors—the lights shined bright in the new hospital. He could hear employees talking and laughing and he felt apprehensive, but didn't feel in danger. Everything seemed normal.

The elevator's stainless steel doors opened, and the nurse pushed him in and turned him around.

Did I just dream this? Am I having deja vu?

Brandon looked behind him at his parents, they smiled. His eyes shifted to the doctor who was typing something on his phone.

The elevator shook briefly, then lifted.

Brandon looked up at the elevator's digital display. The numbers *2, 3,* and then *4,* displayed on the panel. He held his breath as the screen continued displaying the red number *4.*

His dream became clearer, remembering the chaos he had just experienced.

This scared him, but the lights burned bright with no flickering, as in his dream. Everyone seemed okay, no panic, no worries.

Finally, the number *5* displayed, as the elevator came to a stop.

Brandon lowered his head, anticipating the elevator would shake again.

The young nurse smiled down at him, making him feel better.

"Here we are," the doctor said.

The doors opened.

Brandon let out a long breath in relief.

The long, well-lit hallway burst with activity with nurses, patients, and maintenance personnel moving in all directions on its newly polished floor. Halloween decorations filled the lobby and halls. He felt more at ease as the chair moved out of the elevator.

He glanced at the nurse's station, and to his relief, he saw a big number *'5'* mounted in the middle of the reception counter, indicating he was on the *fifth* floor.

He didn't notice no one pushing the wheelchair, as it slowly rolled forward.

Feeling safe and secure, he put the dream he just had further behind him. He almost smiled as he turned to speak to his parents, but saw no one.

No parents, no doctor, no nurse.

Brandon's anxiety and fear quickly returned, and he turned around only to see the elevator doors closing, the light inside flickering. Panic struck him as he tried to get out of the chair. Chains wrapped around his wrists, ankles, and neck, rendering him helpless. The supernatural had returned.

The chair stopped rolling.

Brandon's eyes widened as he screamed at the top of his lungs.

From down the dark hall, the Mangler, dressed in black, ran towards him. He held long chains in both hands, dragging the bloody bodies of his mother and father behind him.

Brandon passed out.

"Brandon? Brandon, how are you feeling?"

He started to come to. He tried to see through his blurry vision. The light hurt his eyes as a hand gently shook his shoulder.

"Hello, Brandon. I'm Denise. I'll be your nurse today," she said.

His vision and thoughts became clearer.

The beautiful young nurse looked at him, smiling.

He wanted to speak, but only managed to slur his words.

His thoughts were clearer than his speech, happily realizing he had only had *another* bad dream.

"Don't worry about talking right now. They gave you a sedative earlier. It might take a little longer to wear off," she said, straightening his pillow.

"Where am I?" he asked, speaking a little clearer, trying to sit up.

Helping him, by raising the bed, she said, "You're at the brand new Bay Coast Health Center. You're one of our first patients." She smiled again.

Everything came back to Brandon now. The old hospital, the new building, built on the same land. His heart rate increased, taking it all in. "How long will I be—"

"You just lay back and relax. We will take good care of you." She paused, her head still down, adjusting the blanket. "Anyone who sees me must die," she said, her voice changed, slower and much deeper now.

The strange voice and her words shook Brandon to his core, his body stiffened.

"Wait . . . what did you just say?!" he asked, frantically leaning over the opposite rail. "Anyone what...?"

"*Anyone who sees me must smile?*" She pointed to the embroidered words on her uniform. "That's our slogan here to keep our patients smiling and hopefully happy. Kinda corny, but..." The nurse smiled, not finishing her sentence.

"If you need anything, just hit the red button. Happy Halloween."

Brandon exhaled, releasing his sudden stress and almost started laughing. He knew now, his mind was playing tricks on him and he was acting paranoid, probably from the medication, but more so from the two nightmares he just had. Maybe, just maybe, this was all behind him now. He laid his head back against the pillow, feeling better.

"Oh, I almost forgot," the nurse said, pausing at the half-open door. The lights flickered in the dark hallway behind her.

"Welcome to Floor Four."

Those four words stunned Brandon. His body tensed again, anxiety taking over, and he quickly closed his eyes, refusing to look.

The Mangler's maniacal laugh echoed in the hall, as the door slowly closed.

Author's Note

In this story, I have taken certain fictional liberties in changing the names of people and places. For anyone who reads this, and for those who live in the town where this story takes place, you may be able to piece together, one chain link at a time, the real places that inspired this novella. If you do locate the old hospital (it still stands, by the way), my advice to you, is to not venture in and explore as the boys did in the story . . . safety concerns, you understand.

But . . . if you do stand at the fence on a quiet night, listen real close. You may hear the unmistakable sounds of a sickle scraping against metal or chains dragging along the stairwell and floors from within. And while you're there, take a glance up at the fourth floor windows. Let me know if you see anyone stirring around up there. If your imagination is anything like mine, maybe you'll write your own scary story.

Now on to more important matters...

What Happened to Brandon?

(scan qr code or visit: **booklaunch.io/acehilink/whtb**)

Purgatory–13 Tales of the Macabre

In the spirit of King, Laymon, Little, and Keene comes a collection of short stories of the macabre. One story begins in the name of research when a world-famous horror author spends the night in one of the most haunted houses around, **Ritter House**, only to discover that reality is much more horrific than fiction. In **Road Trip**, a man must travel across state lines to identify his brother's dead body and drive him home in the back of his car to a mortuary run by a dead man. In **Tic Toc**, a man has two hours to try and prevent a catastrophe in the building that his wife works in, only, he can't recall how or why. His only clue is the nightmare he had two hours earlier. Christmas will never be the same for a little boy in **Santa Claws**, and an old wooden box in a warehouse carries a story all its own in **The Crate**. A trip into **Purgatory** will open the door to these stories and more.

Night Dreams 1 – The Beginning

If you had a gift that allowed you to help others by entering their dreams and nightmares, even if it meant risking their lives, would you use it to stop their suffering?

Joseph Rickettes finds out, as a young boy, he has the gift. Will he help his mother and stop the beast in her nightmares? *The Beginning* tells the story of how it all started for Joseph, and how he came to possess his power, or curse, to delve into and live out, the nightmares of others and how it later plays a part in his adult life as a Dream Psychologist.

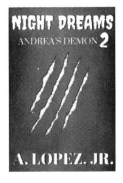

Night Dreams 2 – Andrea's Demon

A backstory of love when Joseph meets Andrea, followed by a happy marriage. But terror-filled, sleepless nights soon take over Andrea's life. She reveals a secret to Joseph about her past and soon their lives spiral further out of control. The haunting novella series continues, with Episode Two answering more questions about Andrea's nightmares and the demon that haunts her. Joseph's gift is severely tested by the demon out to cross over into the real world and take his wife's soul. Joseph battles *his* own demons as his wife, marriage, and life are all put in jeopardy.

Night Dreams 3 – Rising Darkness

The demon attempts to further divide Joseph and Andrea with a relentless mental and physical assault.

Its power may be too much for Joseph to handle alone as he learns more about Andrea's past with her sister, Jessica.

Will Jessica give them the clues and answers they seek?

With nowhere else to turn and with his medical and clinical resources exhausted, Joseph must turn to religion and seek the help of a well-known neighborhood priest, Father Lombardi, for his guidance and experience in dealing with demons, and find the answer to save Andrea's life.

Night Dreams 4 – Tall Man

A fresh start brings a new set of critical decisions for Joseph as the series continues with episode four. Will he help his new patient, Claire Botkins, while knowing the danger in not truly understanding his gift? Claire has a recurring nightmare of being stalked in her own house—a nightmare that tempts Joseph to help her with his unpredictable talents. His motives and decisions could put her in mortal danger. Will his quest to seek revenge against the demon lead him down a one-way road and past the point-of-no-return? Will Father Lombardi attempt to intervene? Joseph starts to second guess himself as he reflects on the past, and his wife, Andrea.

Night Dreams 5 - Malevolence

A secluded lake smothered by a dense, dark forest...a curious boy, a mysterious girl, and a...BEAST!
"Something evil lurks in those woods."
Malevolence introduces new characters into the series, namely, a ten-year-old boy, Michael. His bike rides into the woods opens a door to a fascinating and beautiful world . . . at first. But it is a world he soon wishes, he never unveiled. The only good thing about the woods is, Sarah—a girl he meets, around his age, who tries to help him understand the true meaning of the dark side of the woods. Michael begins to have strange visions and violent nightmares, leading his parents to seek help.

Night Dreams 6 – Soul Reaper

What lives in the lake and woods? The woods turn darker and what dwells there reveals itself, looking to claim more souls and continue its torment on the good people of Patterson Township. Can Michael and Sarah stop it?

Soul Reaper connects the cliffhanger in the fifth episode, and takes us further into the lives of Michael and Sarah and reveals how Joseph begins to lose control of his gift, putting everyone in danger. The three must work together to solve the mystery and evil of the beast stalking Patterson Lake, and the souls taken over the last hundred years. This episode brings us one book closer to the seventh and final episode of the series.

Night Dreams 7 - Underworld

How far will one go to set things right? Nightmares, religion, and other worlds collide in the seventh and final episode in the series. Will science or religion win out? Or is there more to the story than appears on the surface?

In the final episode, Joseph and Father Lombardi battle their own inner demons while trying to prepare for a showdown with the real evil behind the chaos in their lives. Guilt and the need for revenge drive the two men blindly to a fate worse than they could have imagined.

The gates of hell are closer than they think.

FREE DOWNLOAD

"Dreams inspire us, but Nightmares change our lives."

kindle nook kobo
iBooks pdf

NIGHT DREAMS – THE SERIES

GET EPISODE ONE OF THE SEVEN EPISODE SERIES

FREE

★★★★★

Excellent and Suspenseful!!!
Absolutely enjoyed this book, I couldn't stop
reading till I finished it. It's suspenseful and if
you like Freddy Kruger, where you can
connect real life with your dreams then you
will definitely enjoy this!!!
by Judy Tineo - May 7, 2014

Get your free copy of "Night Dreams #1 - The Beginning" when you sign up to the author's
VIP mailing list and FREE newsletter "The Project"
Get Started Here: ⬇

or visit: alopezjr.com for more details

~ In The Works ~

"31 DAYS"
An Apocalyptic Horror Novel

"Tomorrow starts the countdown to Halloween, folks," the radio DJ announced to the listening public. "Yes, tomorrow is October 1st, bringing in the cooler temperatures, shorter days, and the one creepy night of the year that we love so much . . . Beware of the goblins!"

Little did he know that the countdown had already begun, long before he spoke his prophetic words.

The terror that was coming was far more hellish than he, or any of his listeners could imagine. The terror that *is* coming, begins in 31 Days.

About A. Lopez, Jr.

Born and raised in Texas and now residing in Arizona, A. Lopez, Jr. published his first work *Purgatory - 13 Tales of the Macabre* and *Floor Four - A Novella of Horror*, in 2011. He also has the *Night Dreams* Series with seven episodes. His column, 'Ask AJ', appears in the All Authors Magazine, online, and he has had short stories published in Dark River Press, The Sirens Call eZine Issue #14 and the anthologies, State of Horror Illinois by Charon Coin Press and Concordant Vibrancy by All Authors Publishing.

"I chose the Horror genre for the first few books, and have plans to write in different genres with short stories, novellas, and novels." – ALJ

36916173R00064

Made in the USA
Middletown, DE
14 November 2016